Out of Bounds

Out of Bounds

Fred Shank

&

Chris Fisher

To order additional copies of this book, contact:
Xlibris Corporation
1-888-795-4274
www.Xlibris.com
Orders@Xlibris.com
17387

"IF YOU CAN'T ANNOY SOMEBODY,
THERE IS LITTLE POINT IN WRITING."
—SIR KINGSLEY AMIS

FRED AND CHRIS WOULD LIKE TO THANK ALL OF
THEIR FRIENDS WHO MADE THIS POSSIBLE THROUGH
THEIR INSPIRATION, WISDOM AND MOST OF ALL
THEIR PATIENCE. OUT OF BOUNDS COULD NOT HAVE
MADE IT TO PRINT WITHOUT THE WATCHFUL EYE
OF NOSEY NEIGHBOR SHARON, THE ARTISTIC EYE
OF ANDY AND AN EYEFUL OF P. DUPIE.
WE THANK YOU ALL.

Prologue

High atop the basketball court at the center of the arena, the larger-than-life scoreboard showed his team had escaped with a 107-104 victory. The visiting New York Knicks had come from behind to steal a win versus Jerry Stackhouse and the rest of the Washington Wizards, thanks in no small part to a seldom-used shooting guard named Matt Walker. Matt had come off the bench to spark the second-half drive to victory by nailing six out of eight shots for fourteen points, as well as turning in three assists. He gave the Knicks the outside shooting and heady backcourt presence they desperately needed to pull themselves closer to that far too elusive final spot in the playoffs.

"Good job, Casper," a euphoric Wayne Hawkins shouted as the two men jogged off the court into a rain of boos falling from the last row to the very first. "When you come home, you got game."

Matt rolled his eyes at the compliment while moving through the catacombs of the MCI Center en route to the visiting locker room. Wayne was his closest friend on the team, and the starting point guard had been an All-Star more times than Matt could even dream of being in the League.

"Nice touch out there," Knicks Coach Baker said while slipping past the security gate dividing the athletes from the rest of the world. "You gonna bring that with you on Sunday against Philly?"

"I'll try," Matt muttered while hiding the smile that had been steadily building since draining his last jump shot ensuring a New York "W."

For the first time ever, Matt was named the player of the game and was required to do an extra interview for the television broadcast. He was rarely interviewed at all, so to be told that he must spend sometime with the rats, who followed the team's every move on and off the court, was more than welcomed.

Bellying up to his locker, Matt was surrounded by reporters almost immediately. Savoring the fact that he was the flavor of the night, he earnestly answered each and every question with as much humor and personality as he could muster. It had been a long time since he was this high, and he wanted to enjoy it.

But Matt's glee was short-lived as he noticed that he was giving this latest interview less than five feet from the man he replaced on the court—Anthony Michaels. Anthony was a high school phenom who jumped directly from prep school to the professional ranks five years earlier. With his electrifying first step and deadly range spanning twenty-five feet from the basket, Anthony was quickly anointed by the NBA's marketing department as the "next Michael Jordan." He had millions from national endorsement deals with soft drink manufacturers and fast food chains even before his first professional game.

Unfortunately, his skills weren't all what they seemed. With the hard life of a professional baller taking its toll, Anthony couldn't weather the storm of celebrity, and now appeared a shell of the player he had promised to be.

"I'm just thankful for the opportunity I was given to play tonight," Matt said to one of the numerous reporters desperately lunging forward past the crowd of video cameras. "The defense was playing off me and giving me the looks, and tonight, the shots went down."

"Matt, do you think you will start in Philadelphia?" an oafish reporter wheezed from the third row of correspondents.

As Matt searched for the reporter who asked the question, as well as the words to answer it, he saw Anthony shoot him a scornful look while grabbing a towel and heading for the showers.

"Kevin, is that you?" Matt asked as he saw the stumpy reporter for the *New York Post* stumble forward. Shooting a wide smile for the ESPN camera hovering about his locker, he answered, "Come on now, you know that's for the coach to decide."

Matt entertained a few more questions until a nerdy Knicks public relations officer diverted the horde away with promises of a late-night meal from one of the closed restaurants in the arena. As he watched the crowd exit the locker room, Matt sat in his locker with a towel over his shoulder and smiled. He hadn't expected to play a significant amount of time in the game, but when Coach waved him in and didn't send in a replacement, his usual eight minutes turned into a season-high twenty-two.

In previous games, Matt felt largely superfluous as he averaged less than six points and one assist throughout his two-and-a-half-year career. But this night had been different. He was the one who had hit the big shots down the stretch. It was he who made a critical steal to set up the go-ahead score late in the fourth quarter. Finally, he felt like he was a real professional basketball player.

With one last deep breath, Matt snatched a fresh towel and made his way toward the showers. He crept his way through the wave of steam at the beginning of the bathroom tiles before finding nearly all the showerheads deserted. Matt situated himself along the far wall of the group shower, away from two teammates who always seemed to enter into some form of horseplay when they were naked together.

Two shower spaces away from his own, Matt discovered Anthony drowning himself under the rushing showerhead. When he abruptly turned and met Matt's gaze with a heated stare, all the pride and joy he felt from his first real contribution to the team quickly melted away.

The burn from Anthony's stare was strong. Matt felt that its heat was drying the water as instantly as it was hitting his shoulders and chest. He wanted to extend an olive branch. "Damn, I got lucky tonight. I never realized how much Stack would lay off my shot."

Anthony didn't flinch as Matt found himself continuing to downplay his own performance. After Matt had all but said that he lacked any skill at all and should return the nearly six million dollars in salary he had earned since turning pro, Anthony took his towel and exited without turning off his showerhead.

After letting the hot water burn into his aching muscles much longer than usual and much longer than the athletic trainers would have liked, Matt emerged with a white towel draped from his hips exposing his strong and defined upper body.

Anthony was long gone from the locker room. Matt's long shower and senseless babble ensured that, but standing at his locker was Wayne. Wayne had remained in high spirits from the victory. "I can see it in tomorrow's headlines. 'Local boy comes home to slaughter neighborhood team before heading back to high school and pillaging distinguished alumni banquet.'"

"I'm not a *distinguished* alumnus," Matt said dryly as he toweled himself off. "It's just a stupid fund-raiser. I really don't know why I'm going."

"Well, whatever reason it's gotta be good," Wayne said as he slung his garment bag over his large shoulders. "You know, I love the 'W', but did you see Coach? He looks a bit too pissed for the rest of us playin' like shit. I ain't lookin' forward to the flight back to the City. You lucky bastard, you get to stay here, away from the team, and just meet us in Philly."

"I'll trade places with you in a heartbeat," Matt said, hoping that his friend wouldn't take him up on the offer. He didn't mind Coach Baker's constant harassment over the details when it was after a loss, but tonight was a win and Matt was thankful for his get-out-of-jail-free card. Matt wouldn't admit it, but this trip was good for other reasons besides avoiding another earful from Coach.

When his agent arranged this side trip, he was more excited about entering White Hall Academy than anything else in the world. It wasn't because Matt would be able to walk on the basketball court where he became a high school All-American or see the library where he studied to earn his place as valedictorian.

Matt was excited to finally meet and get to know that boy from high school, that boy he knew by name and nearly name alone. Reese Gibbons was, in Matt's memory, a geeky mess and wasn't one of the privileged few who ran with the popular crowd that Matt hung with, if not outright ruled. Even back then, Matt wanted to reach out to Reese. But Matt was too scared and awfully too unaware of his place in the world to act upon his desire. It wasn't until much later that he realized what those feelings were and it was even more time after that where he finally decided to act on them.

"I'm not that 18-year-old who didn't know what I was or what I wanted," Matt thought to himself as he prepared to exit the locker room. Reese had surely transformed in the eight years since their high school graduation and Matt wanted to show that he had changed too. He wanted to scream it, and tell him that their lives were very much the same, just played on different planes. But mostly, he wanted Reese to know that Matt had always noticed him, too.

Chapter One

Tugging frantically upon the zipper on the first of his two carry-on bags proved to no avail, as the bag stubbornly refused to close. "Maybe I don't need a fourth pair of shoes," he said to his marbled English bulldog, Logan, who lay patiently upon his queen-size bed. Tossing his Simple shoes to the back of an overflowing closet, he conceded that his Saucony running shoes, black Prada dress shoes and the Sketchers on his feet were enough to survive the thirty-six hours he was going to be away from his Manhattan apartment.

Looking out the window, waiting for his ride to pick him up to go to the airport, he found his stomach was in knots. It had begun simply enough an hour earlier with a tightening of his chest making his breath harder to come by. Then his stomach began to turn, resulting in him having to lock his knees when he stood to remain stable, which caused his lower back to pulse with pain.

Reese Gibbons was going home, and he wasn't too thrilled about it. Seeing his family was fine, but he was heading back to high school.

White Hall Academy was celebrating its Centennial as the cradle of the nation's elite in its newly refurbished Washington, D.C. campus. Senators, congressmen and bureaucrats alike eagerly positioned themselves to get their respective pride and joy into the hallowed walls snuggled between the District's Rock Creek Park and Georgetown University. Now Reese was asked to walk those halls once again.

Just after popping four Advil and a handful of Tums, there was a familiar ring of his cell phone. "I'm outside, fag," he heard the voice on the other end of the call say.

Taking one last glance into the mirror, Reese noticed that while reaching just shy of six feet and weighing a solid 165 pounds, he was far from the nerdy recluse he had been upon graduation. With soft, dirty blond hair eclipsing his dark brown eyes, Reese was the personification of a late bloomer who often went unnoticed among people who knew him five years ago but could stop traffic with a simple passing of a stranger on the street.

With his two bags slung over his shoulder and Logan's leash in hand, Reese faced the cold, rain-soaked air and raced out the front of his Hell's Kitchen apartment building to Taylor's red Volkswagen Beetle as she wailed away on its horn. "That bitch isn't getting in here," Taylor screamed as Logan hopped into the backseat. "I told you, no."

"But your heart says yes!" Reese sang while Logan moved to the car's backseat looking for a spot to settle. "And you're late, so you owe me. It's only for a night. Plus, he loves you. See how good he's being—and you called him a bitch. Shame on you, can't you see that fine package? He would do any bitch proud."

Rolling her dark brown eyes at Reese's continued praise of Logan's anatomy, she offered, "Fine, but you're picking up the bill for dinner at Pastis next week."

Manhattan was in its typical late winter doldrums with its gray skies and howling winds as Taylor navigated her way onto the 59th Street Bridge. It was hard to believe that the petite creature that was Taylor Sheehan, weighing less than a buck ten and falling short of the five-foot-three mark, could posses such rage behind the wheel.

"God damn these bastards," she exclaimed as a taxi turned left from the right lane tempting her to rub its metal with her own. "Don't they know rubbing isn't racing in New York? You never know who's got a gun in the next car."

"Honey, this isn't LA."

Rolling her eyes yet again and asking herself why she couldn't find any heterosexual men, she asked, "Enough of that. Aren't you excited about this weekend?"

"Honestly, I can't believe I'm going back. My stomach is killing me and all I keep thinking of is how I had no choice in the matter. I mean, with my mom as the chairwoman of the committee and my dad the headmaster. I had to go, but then they invited me to represent my graduating class. That's just torture. It's one thing to go back out of obligation to your parents. It's another one entirely when they ask you to come back on your own merits."

Swerving around a car, which had slowed for its occupants to cast an eye upon Manhattan's ever-changing skyline, Taylor didn't miss a beat. "Oh, don't tell me you don't love it. Showing those people up has been one of your goals since you landed that gig at the *Voice*. Think about all those times when you stumbled home from 'Pop Trash' drunk, dialing me about how you 'would show them.' Damn Reese, every night I prayed for you to find a boy to go home with, just so I wouldn't hear the same tirade every Thursday night at three in the morning."

Taylor rambled on with her theory of why Reese was uneasy about walking the grounds of the Academy once again. She waxed poetically about her communication professor at New York University and his belief of people returning to their defined roles within certain relationships. "You're not the skittish 135-pound, five-foot nothing that you were six years ago when I met you, let alone nothing like what you probably were in high school. But the sad fact is that they will still see you that way."

"Are you trying to cheer me up?" Reese asked in utter disbelief as Taylor confirmed his worst fears.

"I'm just telling you why you're freaking out. It's normal for social misfits to not want to go back to high school," Taylor said as she burst out into howls of laughter.

"I hate you."

Secretly, he was excited about the honor of being asked back to his alma mater. God knew that he wouldn't mind sticking it to a few people. But he also conceded that no matter what he did up North, down in Washington, within the walls of White Hall Academy, he would still be what they saw him as. Labels never change.

"I was the fucking yearbook and newspaper editor, so they expected me to have a stick up my ass," Reese said before adding his own self-deprecating humor. "They just didn't expect me to enjoy that stick as much as I do."

As they approached the passenger drop-off zone at LaGuardia Airport, he said, "Well, thanks for the ride, Tay. I'll give you a ring when I know what time I'll be flying back tomorrow night."

"Good luck! Don't do anyone I wouldn't do," she said with a smirk before speeding away with Logan pressed against the back window, looking horrified at the latest predicament his master had left him in.

Taylor didn't have much to worry about. Reese had pretty much despised nearly everyone who had been at the Academy. He believed that the danger of going to a private school was that differences stood out more in small groups of rich homogeneous kids who felt they were better than everyone else all because they were fortunate enough to travel down the "right" birth canal.

The only person Reese was looking forward to seeing was his senior English teacher, Dr. George Wetherington. Dr. Wetherington was the one who had told him that Reese was destined to write the great American novel. Of course, the great lecturer told one person per year that they possessed that destiny. For Reese, however, it was still a form of validation to be the one who, while not quite there, was well on his way to making his mark on American literary culture as one of the top columnists for New York City's *The Village Voice*.

This quick trip home to the District was also another chance for Reese to visit his parents and see a few school friends who remained in the area. He rarely saw his parents. They would come to New York for conferences in the summer or he would head home for the holidays, but usually the three wouldn't be able to spend more than a meal together. The Gibbons were not on bad terms, and in fact loved and adored each other, All three were highly successful individuals, who were overly committed to their careers and abundant social events. But of course, like most families where everyone is of a certain age, they enjoyed loving each other much more from afar.

After picking up a *New York Post* at the Hudson News in the Marine Terminal for the Delta Shuttle, Reese raced up to one of the e-ticket check-in kiosks. Like most New Yorkers, Reese adored *Page Six*, which served as the *Post's* page of gossip and celebrity sightings from around the City.

As Reese confirmed his reservation, he prayed to slip past security without incident. But it was not meant to be. An overly chipper gate attendant with excessively waxed eyebrows said, "Sir, the computer has selected you to be one of the many passengers who will be randomly searched before boarding this flight."

Reese was certain he saw a kind of twisted glimmer of satisfaction in the eyes of the attendant as he stepped to the side and placed his bag on an examination table. "I hate gay-on-gay crime," Reese seethed to himself.

Another security guard, this one named Rex, was middle aged with a tight graying buzz cut, opened Reese's two bags. To Reese's horror, he remembered there were some necessary supplies packed away to help him survive the weekend and realized Rex was about to find some lube and a small toy that gave him the pleasure his ex-boyfriend, Adam, never could.

A young female security guard passed the wand over his legs as Reese watched Rex continue through his bag. After grunting a few times and cracking a smile, Rex closed up the carry-on and handed it over with a wink of his left eye, "It seems like you have everything you need. Thank you, sir."

Reese chided himself for assuming that in an airport the only person who would be gay would be a flight attendant, not a pair of security guards. When it came to stereotypes, he often dwelled on the situations to determine where his socialization had skewed his view. But ultimately, Reese didn't care. It was given its due time of reflection and quickly forgotten, destined to repeat.

Being the last to board the four o'clock shuttle, Reese found a lone seat between a grandmother painted by Norman Rockwell and an obese businessman, who talked loudly enough on his cell phone to be heard throughout the cabin.

"Excuse me," Reese said while motioning to the empty seat.

"If you don't mind, could you just step across," the elderly woman who sat along the aisle replied. "I've gotten comfortable and my hip is bothering me too much to stand again."

"Of course not," Reese said while trying to work himself and his bags through the nine-inch gap between the woman and the seat in front of her.

Grabbing his *Post* from his bag before stowing it properly under the seat in front of him Reese heard, "Do you live in New York or the District?" Understanding his newspaper would be no form of protection from his new travel companion, he submitted to her required idle banter as the plane prepared for take off.

Reese quickly learned that the elderly woman was named Esther and lived in Northern Virginia with her sister, who couldn't make the trip because a grandchild broke his arm in Colorado. Reese was afraid to ask if the sister went to Colorado or just waited by the phone for the bone fragments to heal.

But, Esther came alone to see her thirty-second showing of the *Phantom of the Opera*. "It was a marvelous production in its day with the original cast of Michael Crawford and Sarah Brightman. The new cast isn't very good, dear, so you shouldn't waste your money to see it. I don't know why I continue to go. Maybe next time I'll see that new one, *The Lion King*."

Reese couldn't believe that anyone could call *The Lion King* the new one or that someone could see *Phantom* thirty-two times. He concluded that *Puppetry of the Penis* and *Naked Boys Singing* would have been too much for Esther to handle. He daringly thought *Aida* and *Cabaret* would have been too edgy for the woman who now had fallen into a merciful sleep clutching her purse and a wad of tissues.

Shortly after the plane was in the air, Reese was able to open his paper to his prized *Page Six*. He fumbled through the usual reports on celebutants Paris and Nicky Hilton, as well as the latest gossip on J. Lo and Ben Affleck. There was another reported outbreak of John Ashcroftism with the Attorney General covering another piece of priceless art with large curtains because he didn't want to look at the sculpture's penis. "Closet case," Reese thought while trying to displace the image of John Ashcroft getting it on with another man.

Finally in the "Just asking . . ." section there was the latest hint of yet another closeted young actor who was parading around town with his beard-slash wife before meeting up with his gay lover in a suite at the Hudson Hotel the same evening.

Reese, who had always believed his sexuality was just a small part of himself, had recently become more militant and found himself resenting celebrities who were gay but publicly denied their sexuality to remain marketable to the Bible beaters in the South and the farmers in the Midwest.

While he could never say for certain that Ricky Martin, Tom Cruise or Mike Piazza were gay, as numerous media reports and the gossip pages had more than alluded to, Reese was smart enough to know that there were hundreds of gay celebrities that hid their sexuality from the public. He strongly believed if more high-profile people came out as homosexuals, there would be less discrimination against all gay men and women.

In fact, during his first year at the *Voice*, Reese had written a column where he outed numerous celebrities. He had confirmed them to possess gay partners or at least numerous affairs with members of their own sex. Of course, his editor, citing "legal" reasons, quickly axed his story. Reese never fully recovered from that blatant act of censoring.

Chapter Two

Reese's parents stood just outside the security exit at Ronald Reagan National Airport waiting for their only child to appear through the glass double doors. Peyton and Alison Gibbons were in their late and mid-fifties, respectively, but didn't look the part. Peyton was tall and lean with lightly salted hair, while Alison's petite frame was overshadowed by her large brown football helmet that had been teased and plastered into place and affectionately termed "the doo."

Alison saw her only child first and rushed forward. "Reese, what's wrong? Do you not know how to turn on your stove or do you simply forget to eat? Doesn't he look *too* thin, Peyton?"

"The boy looks fine," Peyton said as the trio exchanged hugs, handshakes and kisses. Making their way out to the latest parking deck addition, Peyton continued the random and impersonal conversations that were the trend when the Gibbons were together. "Jesus! The irony! Naming this grand airport for the man who fired all those striking air-control workers."

"Isn't his name on the Environmental Protection Agency's building, too?" his wife asked as she settled into the backseat of Peyton's silver Jaguar XJ6 and into her own place of assisting her husband with his sermons one the ills of the day.

Reese loved his parents dearly, but always became annoyed how one of the two would set up the other with nearly laughable and predictable dialogue to follow. He noted his father's favorite rant was on the budget nightmares of the District of Columbia, but Peyton also loved to flex his historical understanding of key historical figures and how their supporters' agendas had attached their names to something as foreign to them as apple pie to the Middle East. He believed the only two appropriately named buildings were the George Bush CIA's Langley headquarters and the J. Edgar Hoover FBI building.

"Maybe only the Intelligence community has the goods on the rest of us, and therefore the wherewithal, to deter the 'powers that be' from putting the wrong name to their buildings," Reese offered to amuse his father. "Just think if the CIA headquarters had Jimmy Carter's name attached to it?"

Peyton's and Allison's charms were a big hit on the local cocktail party circuit, but Reese always found them a bit too rehearsed when his parents broke them out within five minutes of greeting their son at the gate. It almost seemed as if the duo had a checklist of talking points they had to get through before reaching home to find that they had no more to discuss.

A light rain fell over the District as Peyton and Alison, resembling squawking birds more than actual parents, continued on. Peyton directed the car across Key Bridge and to its ultimate destination at the family's town home on the outskirts of Dupont Circle.

Washington was further along in moving out from the grip of winter than New York. The daffodils encircling much of the extensive boxwoods and azaleas in the Gibbons' yard were peaking through the ground with a small number of open blooms among them. A frost was expected in the coming days, but Reese had hoped to have a day or two away from the arctic winds sweeping through the concrete canyons of Manhattan.

"How is Adam?" his mother asked while Reese placed his bags adjacent to the stairs ascending to his childhood room.

"We broke up a few months ago," Reese replied without an ounce of emotion. "It just didn't work. No big deal. When did you paint the living room?"

"Well, if you're not upset about it, we won't be either," she said. "We had it done last month before your father's birthday party. The one you were unable to attend." Her tone dripped of disdain for her only child having to miss his father's birthday.

"I had a deadline. It couldn't be helped."

"Alison be nice to your child," Peyton said while fixing himself a scotch and soda, without the soda. "I opened a bottle of red for you two. I would let it breathe for a few minutes before pouring."

"I am nothing but nice to our child," she said before turning to her son. "I'm sure it's fine. Pour me a glass. It can breathe while I drink it."

"Do you have plans to see Amy while you're in town?" Peyton asked as Reese prepared two glasses from his father's extensive collection of South American wines.

Amy was Reese's best friend before moving off to college. The two were inseparable from the moment they met at age six. As two only children rarely do, the two quickly bonded, but only on Amy's terms. She was undoubtedly the older sibling in the relationship and often would point out her two-month seniority in age throughout their childhood. She told Reese when to play and when to pout, but she also served as his protector, willing to fight off dissenters to her voice and mockers of Reese's obvious "differences." Amy looked to him for humor and balance from her all-too serious personality. It was an easy existence, if now, only in small doses.

"I wrote her an e-mail last week," Reese said. "She didn't respond."

"Well, I'm sure she's very busy," Alison said. "I read her articles everyday. She now covers Capital Hill for *The Washington Post*."

"I heard through the grapevine," he lied. Amy served as his only connection to his former friends in the District. In truth, Reese read Amy's articles nearly as often as he read his own. The Internet is a wonderful thing.

"But what about your stories?" Peyton inquired as he moved the trio into the kitchen and he started the grill on the back deck. "Any movement on a book deal?"

"I spoke to another publisher two weeks ago, but he just wanted a date," Reese said. "My neighbor Sharon thinks she can get me in at one of the bigger publishing houses. One of her clients at the spa she opened is an assistant to somebody or something like that. I'm not holding my breath."

"Well, that would be fantastic," he said to his son. "Your columns could be easily marketed in a compilation, especially with all the trash on the market nowadays."

"I would love to be able to give my son's book away as gifts," Alison offered.

"That's always been an option, but I'm in no rush to put something like that out there," Reese said while turning a deaf ear to his father's backhanded compliment and his mother's ego. "I would rather pursue that once I have my first novel published. It's a bit backwards, I realize. I don't want to be one of those columnists who just republish their work for a fast buck."

"Selling out has become the standard in this society," Peyton conceded. "It seems like you've thought about it a great deal. Your plan sounds like a good one, too." Reese was always amazed to find that his parents acted more surprised than expected when it came to their son's competence.

As the steaks grilled away under Peyton's watchful eye, the Gibbons caught up on the lives of aunts, uncles and cousins, the bizarre movements of neighbors, and of course the Centennial Celebration at White Hall Academy.

"My dream is to have the generations come together and foster a connection outside the Academy and bring the White Hall camaraderie to New York, Los Angeles and wherever our alumni live and breathe," Alison said while the evening's alcohol allowed her to see utopia more clearly.

Hours later when carafes of wine had run dry and the food had more than settled Reese retired for the evening. Finding his room just as he had left it, in its nearly perfect early 1990's state, he quickly fell into his flannel-lined double bed dressed in his cashmere pajama pants from Barney's warming his body.

With a poster of Marky Mark clutching his Calvin's gracing the back of his bedroom door, Reese began to do what every teenage boy does in his childhood room before slipping into a drunken slumber.

*   *   *

The phone pierced through the morning quiet of the Gibbons' house shortly after nine. Hearing its fourth ring, Reese recalled his parents' planned early departure. He stumbled to the phone resting in the upstairs foyer.

"Hello," he said with sleep muffling his voice.

"Hey, troll. Did I wake you?" Amy chirped, giving way to her insomniac nature. Reese was always aware of Amy's inability to grasp the most important lesson of adolescence, learning the love of sleep.

"Yeah, but it's OK," he said, clearing his throat. "I was wondering when I would hear from you."

"I totally forgot about it, until my mother called this morning to remind me. Apparently, on their morning walk your mother mentioned that your arrival had gone unnoticed by myself."

"Gotta love Alison," Reese said with a slight chuckle. "Tattling has always been her favorite pastime. But, what are you up to?"

"I have an interview this morning on the Hill and another late in the afternoon."

"Anything good?"

"The farm bill. So not really," Amy replied. "You want to do lunch around one at the usual place?"

"Done. See you then."

Hanging up the phone, Reese thought about how easy it was to talk to Amy. Despite the two friends never spending any time of consequence together over the past five years, she was still comfortable.

In the kitchen, Reese a found freshly cut grapefruit in the fridge and biscuits kept warm in the oven. He brewed coffee as he spent the rest of the morning, devouring the different sections of his parents' four daily newspapers.

Shortly before heading out the door for a quick jog around the neighborhood, Reese's cell phone sang its familiar song. "How's my baby?" he asked as he could hear Logan barking in the background. "Seems like someone didn't sleep well."

"Reese, you are a pig from hell," Taylor shouted in reference to her love of Ms. Weezer in *Steel Magnolias*. "He snored all night long and stole the covers."

"Sounds like your usual date. Who said you two wouldn't hit it off?" he asked while trying not to laugh. "But the big question is; did he shit the floor?"

"Yes! And he ate through my Manolo strappy slingbacks!"

"Oh, you'll buy another pair. It's not like Daddy can't afford it," Reese said, trying hard to hold back the laughs. "Plus, Logan only steals the covers when he wants you to get up and take him out. He's not crazy. Just pay attention to him."

"Whatever," Taylor said in resignation. "How have you been?"

Reese filled her in on his parents' latest antics before heading out the door for his obligatory five-mile trek through Rock Creek Park. He found physical exertion to be the key to a happy visit home, and with last night going as smoothly as it did, he didn't see why he should skip the jog and remain restless until that night's Centennial Celebration.

The main parks of New York City and Washington couldn't have been more telling tales of each city's attempt at running itself. Central Park, after battling back from mismanagement in the 1970s and '80s, was now safe, clean and the jewel of Manhattan, while Rock Creek Park was far from it. Growing wild and virtually unchecked with deep ravines cutting through the sprawling layout, Rock Creek Park was a haven for hustlers, drug pushers and other blights upon society.

As Reese rambled through the running paths near the park's Pierce Mill, he stumbled upon one of the many picnic areas. This one in particular was one where he would spend hours as a child. Amy and he played all the great dramas of the 1980s from *Falcon Crest* to *Dynasty*. But his favorite was *Dallas*. Reese played JR to Amy's *Sue Ellen*. As Sue Ellen, Amy would take leaps in character and always hide a water gun in an attempt to shoot JR. Reese would plead that Sue Ellen never shot JR, but Amy always successfully argued, "Well, she should have." From there the game would deteriorate to the day's end of playtime before the two would journey back home after a quick stop over at Henry's ice cream shop.

Reese gently smiled to himself as the *Dallas* theme song played in his head. He scanned the ground looking for other memories from his childhood. The curved tree line along the edge of the picnic area was Southfork, while the covered picnic area served as the corporate headquarters of Ewing Oil.

He laughed to his own delight at the trivial, yet devoted dreams of a child. The simplicity was its genius. There were no arcs of character. There were no lessons learned. The cowboy with the white hat was always good, and JR was always bad, even when he got shot.

A light spring rain began to fall as Reese turned toward home and thoughts of his not-too distant childhood rushed in and out of his mind.

*   *   *

Amy was situated in a back booth at a diner along Wisconsin Avenue. This obscure out-of-the-way diner was their diner and it was considered by the two friends to be their semiprivate grazing area since it lacked any connection to the Academy. The two friends eagerly met each other with hugs and kisses in genuine excitement to see each other.

"How was your morning?" Amy asked.

"I read the *New York Times* for the front page, the *Wall Street Journal* for the market report, the *USA Today* for the Life section and the *Post* for politics," Reese said with wry grin. "But the big news is that I found the old space in Rock Creek Park where we used to play *Dallas.* I just stumbled upon it."

"How did it take me ten years to tell you that you were gay?" she asked rhetorically, in reference to the summer before their junior year at the Academy when Amy encouraged Reese to accept and embrace his love of men.

"I did deny that I was gay," Reese said smiling. "I just didn't want to give you the satisfaction."

"Everyone in this town denies everything," Amy argued. "But we all know the truth and I knew it back then. I just didn't have the vocabulary for it until we were older."

"Have you got the vocabulary now?"

Ignoring Reese, Amy continued, "It's amazing how as a child, something can be obvious, yet not have a label."

The friends fell into their usual update conversation: Who was dating whom? Why parents are insane? And, their favorite, why men suck?

"You're in town for the Centennial, right?" Amy asked knowing full well the answer. Reese feared that she was hurt by the lack of her own selection, but knew even if invited, she would never attend.

"Yeah. It's in five hours, actually. I'm not looking forward to it."

"Who's going besides you?"

"I heard that Matt Walker is the other one from our class."

"Wow, the prom king and the yearbook editor. Did you hear that he is gay? How ridiculous is that? Wasn't he fucking all the girls in our class, except for me of course?"

"Yeah, it's ridiculous. He's not gay. He's in the NBA."

"But, he's not married," she argued.

"You aren't either," Reese said without thinking of Amy's cancelled wedding from the past summer. Trying to regain his footing, he offered, "Plus we're only twenty-five, Amy. None of us should be getting hitched. Of course, I'm not allowed to be."

"We're not talking about you," Amy said in her pit bullesque style of conversing. "I'm not agreeing with the rumors anyway, they're made up by bitter fags like you who just want to 'out' celebrities for their own cause. But for the sake of argument, just because he plays in the NBA doesn't mean that he doesn't suck cock."

"You've got to be kidding me. Matt Walker. Our class president. A basketball All-American, both in high school and college. Yeah, he's gay!" Reese said rolling his eyes more times than he thought was humanly possible. Continuing, Reese mocked his own kind by asking, "Why are they trying to out someone who isn't gay? Shouldn't they be outing all the gay boy band members? Those are the ones who really are into the funky butt love."

"Isn't gay boy band member redundant?"

Chapter Three

The Centennial Committee for White Hall Academy spared no expense for its lavish celebration. With two successful alumni chosen from every five-year "generation," the school was overflowing with activity when Reese arrived for the celebration dinner and the accompanying dedication of its new theater wing.

Quickly noticing Matt Walker from across the room, Reese thought of what a perfect choice he was for one of the selections. Matt was an outstanding student while at the Academy, and more importantly, had gone on to a successful basketball career garnering him household-name status. A two-time All-American at Stanford University, who led them to their first Final Four in a lifetime, he was a seventeenth selection in the National Basketball Association's Rookie Draft. While his professional career with the New York Knicks had not taken off, his guaranteed multimillion-dollar contract had given him the freedom to pursue other interests.

Matt served on three Board of Directors for children-based charities and had just opened *the* hot new art gallery on the Lower East Side with Robert De Niro. It was also rumored that he was seeking out investors for a restaurant to go in the development on the site of the former World Trade Center. He was a jack-of-all-trades and appeared to be a master of them all.

Reese, on the other hand, was believed to be a controversial pick by the Centennial Committee. The fact that he was the son of two of the five committee members made his selection look self-serving. In actuality, both his father and mother had reclused themselves from the selection process in Reese's case. The other three Committee members unanimously voiced their support for the young writer from New York, to whom awards were quickly and steadily coming.

He initially came to the public's attention when a writing assignment in his communication theory class at New York University turned into a feature in *Out* magazine. Reese's critical examination of human sexuality as defined by pop culture landed him in the hot seat on numerous talk shows and other pseudo news programs hosted by Bill O'Reilly and Rush Limbaugh. He had argued that there was a direct correlation between the 1990s fitness craze and its effect on male self-concept and sexuality. Ultimately he concluded that a more prominent gay culture and, perceived, population had been born. Of course, Reese never thought that he was the antichrist the pundits made him out to be. But he repeatedly stood on their firing line to fight their agendas.

Reese believed his success in New York would never be seen at the Academy outside the Committee's desire to get as many reputable names at its banquet. He figured he would still be thought of as the same son of the Headmaster who never quite fit in. While Matt was the Academy's proud son, Reese knew no matter what his triumphs were outside the Academy, he would always be their illegitimate child.

"I read your column every week," Matt said with a friendly smile while reaching for a stuffed mushroom from the tray a well-built waiter was passing through the Academy's library.

Reese stumbled through his glass of red wine, while the former high school All-American continued. "It cracks my shit up. Actually most of the guys on the team have started following it. Our equipment manger is required to get copies of the *Voice* for us when we're on the road."

"I didn't know my writing was required reading in the NBA," Reese replied dryly, taking another sip of his wine.

"It isn't. It's an entertaining and insightful read. Isn't that the point?" Matt inquired, hoping to draw his prey onto the playing field. "Most of the guys liked the one you wrote last year on the orthodox Jew and his stripper girlfriend. Of course, many of the guys saw her work before she was so infamous."

Reese recalled a news item when four of the Knicks—absent Matt—were accused of securing prostitutes through a popular strip club in Manhattan. Reese could only imagine long-time Knick and New York icon Patrick Ewing sitting alongside an orthodox Jew from Westchester County panting for some pussy. Men are always slaves to their dicks, he concluded.

"Yeah, I heard people within your profession show a certain loyalty to that industry."

Noticing the slight dig against athletes, Matt just smiled and replied, "We're not all like that."

Reese's mind began to race; why was he so off-center? Matt was being nice. Why resort to being the skinny sixteen-year-old loner in high school and become overly defensive? That wasn't him anymore. Be nice, he commanded.

At the same time, Matt was wondering whether Reese's animosity was heartfelt or just reactionary. He had encountered one too many jaded guys in his life that resented successful athletes since they were largely considered stupid and spoiled.

But before Reese could try to mend his earlier gaffe, Patricia Wyatt came strolling along from across the library. Ms. Wyatt was the Academy's saucy French teacher and all-around jovial character.

"Bonjour!! Bonjour, mes étudiants!" she exclaimed.

As she continued to babble on, Matt and Reese perceived Ms. Wyatt's obvious happier disposition since earlier in the evening when she had been cornered by a few of the social science teachers. She had been hired in Matt and Reese's sophomore year and was relatively closer in age to her students than most of the other esteemed faculty.

"C'est bon de vous voir les garçons," she continued. "Ou, je dois dire des hommes! Vous a grands . . . y forts."

Neither man could understand a word of Ms. Wyatt's ramblings, but the picture cleared when she rubbed Matt's right bicep with her left hand and brushed against Reese's tight ass with her right forearm.

Matt softly moved his hand to Ms. Wyatt's and began to talk of playing the French national team at the World Championships in Rome. "I had a horrible game because one of their forwards kept shouting 'Les américains aiment sucer le pénis.'"

"Oh my!" Ms. Wyatt replied while looking down in embarrassment, but catching a glance at Matt's bulging crotch before she continued, "Did your teammates realize what they were saying?"

"A few did, but that was because it sounds so similar to the English translation."

"Does that happen often in games?" Reese inquired.

"From time to time," Matt said. "Unfortunately trash talking is part of the game. That's also the nature of today's athletes. We all feign interest in the arts and higher education for public relation purposes, but we are—for the most part," casting a glance at Reese, "today's Roman gladiators."

"Well, hopefully you won't be fighting to the death in your next game," Ms. Wyatt said, flashing her brilliant smile. "I do believe that the party is needing to move down into the new wing. Have you two seen the theater addition?"

Neither Matt nor Reese had yet found their way to the new Patriots Hall, where the night's festivities would continue. Ms. Wyatt continued speaking of the Academy's large commitment to the Arts, but also the "dreadful" construction noise and parking headaches for the students and staff.

"I'm sure the Academy had to make amends in one way or another for all the students' Mercedes being covered in dust," Reese mocked.

"You laugh, but those kids complain about anything and everything. I do believe that the lacrosse team earned a small fortune, washing cars on Friday afternoons."

The trio tried to laugh off their truth about the current youth that seemed to fill not only White Hall Academy but the nation as a whole. "I knew we were spoiled brats," Matt considered, "but this seems a bit out of hand."

Ms. Wyatt was notably quiet to Matt's attempt to distance himself from the elitist youth of today as they entered Patriots Hall. She had always thought every student that walked through the door of the Academy was an elitist brat, who should have gotten on their knees every day and thanked God for placing them in such a warm and secure womb.

Despite Reese's parents' obvious involvement in the night's festivities, he was shocked to find himself in a setting that should have been so familiar but in actuality seemed quite foreign to him. His father was talking to a congressman and his young female companion by a bay window, while his mother greeted guests at the entry table where seating assignments were distributed.

His mother tossed Reese's seating card over to him while not skipping a beat from a conversation with Dr. George Wetherington, the English department chair, as well as Reese's first mentor. Reese saw he was assigned to table five but waited to talk to his former teacher.

"Reese, it's so great to see you," exclaimed Dr. Wetherington. "You know I keep track of your writings from the clips your mother has in her office."

"I didn't know she did that. And all this time I thought she was ashamed of my low-brow perceptions on society," he said showing his embarrassment of his mother's constant fawning from afar. "But how are you doing, Dr. Wetherington?"

"I'm just fine, and do not think for one second that your writing is low brow. Walter Winchell was one such man who was accused of butchering and dumbing down the language and popular perceptions, but he spoke to the people. That is the highest compliment any writer can have."

The two continued talking of the past and many of the developments in Reese's career until the bell rang and the crowd made their way to its seats.

Finding his eight-top table in the middle of the second row from the podium, he quickly noticed younger faces. The tables had obviously been arranged to have each generation segregated from the other.

"So much for meeting the past," Reese said to no one in particular.

Matt was already seated at his table, as were a man and woman in their late twenties whose faces were familiar, but not known by the young writer. Sitting down next to Matt, Reese offered, "Hello, I'm Reese Gibbons, Class of 1995."

Matt had been worried that Reese had changed table assignments when they drifted away from each other entering Patriots Hall. But Matt had decided to play it cool and just be a bit more than friendly throughout the night. Hopefully, Reese would bite.

"Henry, we're being invaded by freshmen," an attractive blond said while forcing a smile from her clenched teeth. "Welcome Reese. I'm Johanna Tates and this is Henry Roberts. We're both Class of 1992."

"Nice to meet you both."

"I'm a fellow at John Hopkins Hospital, while Johanna works on Senator Thompson's staff on the Hill," Henry offered.

"What do you do, Reese . . . besides be invited to these functions out of obligation?" Johanna quipped.

"Reese writes a popular column for *The Village Voice* in New York City," Matt interjected just short of proud.

"Is that one of those community papers?" she smirked.

"It's not exactly the town paper with birthday party and wedding announcements," Reese explained. "But it's definitely a local New York City paper."

"Oh, that's cute," she said, letting herself wrap her thought around such a novel career choice. "Does your piece run on the page with all those faggot hooker ads or is it on the page behind that?"

Too stunned to reply, Reese heard Matt come to his defense yet again, "Any community would be lucky to have the *Voice*. I believe over one million people read it every week. And pardon the pun, but the paper is the voice of the City. Reese's column is one of its top features. Nearly everyone on the Knicks reads his work."

"I'm sorry . . ." Johanna offered while Reese was more than taken aback by the confrontation playing out at table five.

"Yes, you are," Matt said, raising his voice. "But that's OK, since you're obviously from Montana. That is where Senator Thompson is from, correct? I'm sure you have much in common with his constituents since you were born and raised here in the District and attended the Academy. And didn't you go to Georgetown? But, let me ask, have you ever been to Montana? Could you even find it on a map?"

With the table deafened by the silence, Matt continued with a sneer toward Johanna, "Great fly fishing. I go once a year with my father."

"Excuse me," Johanna mumbled, as she retreated from the table.

"Don't mind her," Henry said. "She's just a bit tired from working on her back and knees all day for Senator Thompson."

The table broke out in laughter and maintained a light friendly vibe through a dinner of chimney tuna steaks, grilled portobello and squash salad. Between dinner and dessert, Peyton Gibbons took the podium and embarked on his story as headmaster for the past twenty years, bringing certain notice to high-powered alumni who gave thousands to the Academy annually.

Reese was taken aback by his father's natural presence as he worked the crowd. Both earlier in the library and now, the elder Gibbons seemed warm and open. Reese could not help but notice how much of a polar opposite he was to his father. Nowhere on Peyton could cynicism and jade be found. A bit of envy crept upon Reese.

As his father concluded Reese asked, "When are you headed back to the City?"

"I'm going to train it to Philadelphia," Matt replied. "We have a game there tomorrow."

"Oh, I thought we could share a cab back to National Airport tonight, if you were going to take the shuttle," Reese offered to Matt's delight.

"The last shuttle of the night leaves in ten minutes," Harry interjected. "They've cut down on the flights in and out of that airport since September eleventh."

"That changes your plans," Matt concluded. "There is an express train in an hour that ends up in Penn Station. I'm taking that one to Philly."

"I haven't taken the train in years, but it looks like my only option if I don't want to spend the night at my parents' house again. God knows, that would be fun," Reese said with a mischievous grin.

"See, your choice is obvious. I have a car picking me up in thirty minutes if you want to join me," Matt said, hoping and praying that his old classmate would take him up on the offer.

Watching Reese contemplate his options, or lack there of, Matt thought of what a great opportunity he had been handed. A shortened shuttle schedule and the opportunity to be the hero while playing the unexpected ally alongside Reese at the dinner table couldn't have been planned better. A car and train ride was more than he could have ever dreamed.

As the crowd began to break up at the conclusion of the evening, Reese approached his parents and told them that he was heading back to New York that evening.

"I wish you could stay," Peyton pleaded. "It seems we never see you anymore."

"Peyton, don't give your son a hard time. You know that it's just as much our busy schedules as it is his that keeps us apart," Alison said. "But your father is right, Reese. We don't see you enough. Let's try to work on that in the future."

"Thanks, Mom. I agree. You two take care and I'll call you next week."

Heading out the door after quickly gathering his bags from his father's office, Reese thought of what a pleasant surprise the evening had been. He had thought he was walking into a beehive and he was nearly right. But never in his wildest dreams would Reese have thought that Matt Walker would come to his rescue or that the former high-school star could be so witty, charming and attractive.

Standing at six-feet, five-inches and weighing 210 pounds according to NBA.com, Matt was a lean yet powerful physical specimen. His dark, choppy hair and piercing blue eyes worked all too well with his chiseled jaw and nearly constant smile. Reese found him more attractive now, than when the two were in the group shower one glorious afternoon at the conclusion of track and basketball practice. That image had been the mental picture Reese used frequently for nearly ten years to help him "relax."

"Nothing like a late-night train," Matt said as they settled into the backseat of the Town Car he had ordered. "You know I've traveled more than I care to ever think about, but the train gets me every time."

"The train?"

"Yeah, there is just this romantic undertone to it. Like those classic photographs from the World Wars with the soldiers leaving to fight and their wives or girlfriends gathering goodbye kisses or merely looking on. I love those classic shots. The emotion of it is so striking. And don't get me started on the architecture of these great stations. This one, Union Station, has one of the most beautiful entry halls I have ever seen."

Reese began to melt into his leather seat as Matt continued his romantic monologue on a random piece of Americana with the same passion he took onto the basketball court each and every night for the Knicks.

"Think about all the reunions and tearful goodbyes that have occurred in the train stations across this country," Matt continued. "All the people who saw people for the last time or were seeing them for the very first. These places are treasures."

"I don't want to burst your bubble," Reese said, "but can't you say the same things about an airport?"

"No way! First, those places are so crowded and loud. In an airport, there are always people screaming about their seat assignments or delayed flight or missing luggage," he said before turning to meet Reese's eyes. "But most importantly, have you ever had a great kiss in an airport?"

Apparently the question was not rhetorical as Matt stared at

Reese, waiting for a response. The intensity was something Reese was not expecting as he tried to respond. He only was able to muster an "uh, uh" while shaking his head from side to side.

"See, I didn't think so. The environment just isn't conducive for a good kiss, let alone a great one. A train station kiss would be nice, though."

The two rode in silence for the remaining five blocks to the station as Reese tried to control his growing erection.

"We have ten minutes to catch the train," Matt said as they entered the station. "Do you want anything to eat? I can grab something, while you pick up your ticket."

"I think I'm fine. But, thanks anyway."

"OK, I'm going to grab something. Meet you at the gate," Matt said as he nearly skipped away from Reese before catching himself, acting too enthusiastic to his unexpected good fortune.

Walking through the station and getting his ticket, Reese could not imagine spending the next two hours alongside Matt without cumming all over himself. "Relax. Act like you're not the freak you know you still are," he told himself.

There was no line at the gate when Reese arrived with ticket in hand.

"I got some beers for the ride," Matt said as they handed their tickets to an overjoyed Amtrak worker trying to play it cool since he recognized he was in the presence of an NBA player.

"Oh, all right," Reese said uneasily, not knowing if he could trust himself with any more alcohol in his system. "Did you get that kiss you were hoping for?"

"No, but a guy offered me a blowjob in the restroom."

"You wouldn't need that beer if you took him up on his offer."

"What makes you think I didn't accept?" Matt said with a devilish grin.

Chapter Four

They settled into the fourth car of Amtrak 198, which was bound for Boston, and as the train slowly began to roll out of Union Station Matt cracked open a couple of beers. Matt hoped that Reese's lesser build would make him more susceptible to the influences of the six-pack he persuaded from the lonely bartender at Union Station.

"Want a Heineken?" Matt asked as he forced the beer into Reese's hand and failing in his attempt to play it cool.

"So, you've been in New York since leaving White Hall, right?" Matt asked as he took a tug on his first beer of the night.

"Yeah, I went to NYU with all the other gay boys," Reese said, wanting to establish that he wasn't ashamed or attempting to hide his sexuality. Although, his writing dealt with it on a near weekly basis, throwing the first stone into the conversation would cause an abrupt ripple, but hopefully help with smoother sailing later in the evening. "It's like in its University recruitment brochures it says, 'If you suck dick, come to NYU. Our ratios are reversed.'"

Matt rolled into an uneasy laughter and crossed his left knee with his right ankle before taking the bait. "Ratios?"

"You know, that whole Kinsey study, where he concluded that ten percent of the population is gay. Well, at NYU I believe ten percent of the male population is straight. So therefore the ratios are reversed from the rest of society."

Reese fired off all sorts of reasons of why young boys from across the country flock to the West Village to expand their asses, as well as their minds. Matt was content to just sink back into his seat and listen intently to the young columnist, whom he never really got to know in high school, ramble on and on. "Since it was New York," Reese continued, "and no one seemed to care. I decided to come out. I started going to bars, lounges and clubs. Then somewhere along the way, I was finally able to be the guy who I knew I was. I have to thank NYU for that, just as much as I do for the sheep skin hanging on my apartment's wall."

"Sounds as if your college experience was very different from my own," Matt offered. "I'm kind of jealous."

"Jealous? God, why? You became a household name at Stanford for hitting that shot to go to the Final Four. It was only Kentucky's improbable comeback that gave them the national title and not you."

Matt kept that he loved the fact that Reese followed his career to himself. "You knew I did that?"

"It was kind of hard to miss. You were on television for the entire month of March and with New York's weather always blowing donkey in the spring, I usually fall into a pattern of heavy TV watching for my column. But still I can't imagine how you managed to stay so normal with all that exposure."

"Normal is a strong word, but I've tried to live a balanced life off the court," Matt said as he continued to expand on the daily routine of media engagements and other promotional duties he endured while in college. "I just remember how my dad kept saying that college would be the best time of my life."

"It wasn't?"

Matt took a long swig of his quickly disappearing beer before answering, "I hope not. Sometimes, I think it would have been just better to be Matt Walker, Steven and Hannah's son; not Matt Walker, basketball star."

"I can understand that, although I don't believe it," Reese replied with a jab of his elbow to the side of Matt's tight torso. "I mean, you're a fucking millionaire at age twenty-five. On top of that, you got a free ride at a great university, and obviously, learned something while you were there besides an outside jump shot.

Plus, you're entirely too easy on the eyes. Unfortunately, Matt, you are the personification of having it all."

"You don't honestly believe that I have it all, do you?" Matt asked, listening to Reese's praise of his physique echo in his head. "I live on the road. I have no family of my own and I can never tell if people like me for me or for my status and money."

"I'm sorry about your parents," Reese said on a somber note, giving respect to Matt's ordeal as a freshman in college when a car wreck took the only family he had ever known.

Matt's head hung low as he took another drink from his bottle. Reese fell into an awkward silence that he wished he had avoided, but there was nothing else to say. So he stole a page from his parent's conversation handbook and kept the conversation moving and in his direction.

"Well, you might not have it all, but you're closer to it than I am," he pleaded. "I'm the one who has been on the outside, looking in all my life."

"Were you gay in high school?" a befuddled Matt asked as he opened two more beers for the only people awake on the designated "quiet" car.

"I've always been gay," Reese said flatly. "I just didn't have a label for it until I was in high school. God knows I had heard kids call other kids fag—especially when it was directed at me. Children in elementary school can be brutally honest."

"Both perceptive and cruel!" Matt interjected as Reese continued.

"Around my sophomore year at the Academy, I started realizing that I wasn't just looking at some of the cuter guys with just admiration like 'Oh, I want a chest like that.' It became more of 'I would love to touch that chest.' Then I concluded I wanted to do things to those boys that my other friends were saying about the girls."

"Any of those 'cute boys' you mentioned on the basketball team?" Matt asked with an inquisitive yet taunting look. As soon as the words left his lips, he recoiled in slight shock at his brash approach since the two were now alone.

"Sorry, you weren't my type," Reese replied with a laugh and another elbow jab at Matt's torso. "I was more about people like Chris Koehler and the other guys on the soccer team. Those guys had a particular style and weren't accompanied by the 'big man on campus' complex that most of the basketball team possessed."

"I was not a conceited asshole in high school. I was nice to people," Matt said defensively. He wondered if Reese really thought he was this way or just getting him back for being popular more than eight years ago.

"I'm not saying that you were mean. But try real hard to remember a single time you ever spoke to me, other than to inform me that I had gotten a statistic wrong in the sports section of the newspaper or yearbook," Reese reasoned.

Reese sat back catching, Matt squirm in his seat. Of course, Matt remembered the time the two shared the group shower after their respective practices. But Matt wasn't about to recall that piece of information in a now-reawakened train car from its noisy stop in Wilmington. Finally, he took a long drag from his near-empty beer before exhaling strongly and twisting his lower lip while shifting his left shoulder closer to his ear.

"See, you can't!" Reese said in satisfaction. "You, along with most everyone else on the 'big three' sports teams, barely knew I existed. It's not like I'm pissed about it. Hell, it was in high school. I'm just saying you were going to be the last group of people in that school that I was ever going to be attracted to."

"I can accept that. We were a pretty cocky bunch," Matt conceded but still upset with himself about letting Reese think that he never noticed him. "So you were 'out' in high school. I had no idea. I thought you were dating that chick, Amy."

"God no!" Reese exclaimed as a few of the passengers turned to show their dissatisfaction coming from the drinking duo. "Amy's a smart girl and made a play for me once, but she knew what I was before I did."

"What do you mean? Did she tell you that you were gay?"

"I don't like to give her too much credit, but yes, she did,"

Reese said while finishing his beer. "Around our junior year she just came out and said 'Reese, you like dick, don't you?' She's kind of brash that way, so I freaked out and denied it. She was too much of a good friend to flat out reject my denial, but she knew. She just became more sly about it all through our last years at the Academy. She started dropping little comments about how hot guys were when we'd pass them out and about. It took me until my first break from college to confirm her suspicions."

"Damn."

"It's a coming out story," Reese said rather dryly. "It wasn't until I got to NYU and had the opportunity to be exposed to so many different types of people, as well as take advantage of being around all the other great aspects of living in a city like ours from the museums, plays, architecture, and of course, the nightlife."

"Wait! You're an architecture fan?" Matt exclaimed.

"Yeah, I always liked it," Reese answered while noticing Matt was becoming more than excited about the new topic of discussion. "I mean growing up in the District with all those white marbled buildings, and then moving to New York, which is a melting pot of grand old buildings and fresh modern marvels, I don't see how anyone couldn't find it interesting."

With all the giddiness of a young schoolgirl who has a new lollypop and jump rope, Matt came out of his seat demanding, "You have to tell me what your favorite structure in New York is right now."

Now looking at his traveling companion as if he was some bizarre, comic-relief character imported from a Disney movie, Reese answered meekly, "I guess the Chrysler building. It's so big and shiny."

"Oh, the gargoyles are nice," Matt offered before launching into an explanation of why he couldn't choose the Chrysler or the Empire State buildings. "So many people just default to the Empire State when the only thing interesting about it is the old dirigible-mooring tower on top. That, and its lights. I just can't choose either, they're too cliché. I would have to choose . . ." Matt wondered to himself if he was babbling too much, but was fearful of falling into an awkward silence. "The Brooklyn Bridge is amazing, but so is the Guggenheim and Grand Central Station."

"You really do like architecture, don't you?" Reese said with genuine intrigue. "I thought you were just being smooth in the car on the way to the station."

"Yeah, I love it almost as much as I do basketball," Matt said, now opening the duo's fourth beer. "I always wanted to be an architect, if the basketball thing never worked out."

"Thankfully, it did and you're in the NBA."

"Yeah, I made the League," Matt said, trying to be downbeat. "But I'm still on my first contract, it's not like I'm guaranteed a career. But at least with all my travels. I've gotten to see a lot of amazing architecture. Hell, the Philadelphia City Hall is one of my favorites. You know the building, right?"

"I guess I've seen pictures of it, if that's what you mean?" Reese offered. "Somehow, though, I've never actually visited Philadelphia. No, that's a lie. I was on a field trip in the third grade and all I remember from that is Tommy Hicks pushing me into the mud and laughing."

Not being able to picture the adult version of Reese allowing someone to push him around without some sort of retaliation, Matt ventured to skip the obvious follow-up question and stay on message. "Let me tell you something. I own a gallery and we have exhibits of architectural photos way too often for my taste. But, you know why? They're all crap. Structures are built to be experienced first hand and not from a glossy black and white photograph any kid in junior high can snap."

"Remind me not to purchase any more prints of Ansel Adams," Reese humored.

"He did landscapes, not architectural structures. But look, I have the perfect idea," Matt said and detailed his plan for Reese to get off the train in Philadelphia, stay the night and see City Hall, as well as some other historical places. "So, then at the end of the day, if you're not covered in mud from Tommy Hicks, you're going to come to my game versus the 76ers on one of my tickets."

"Well, that's an offer," Reese said uneasily rolling his eyes. "I would be able to see two things I've never seen before."

"You're not trying to tell me that you've never been to a Knicks game, are you?" Matt said in disbelief. "You live in New York City, you write a pop culture column, I'm on the team, and you've never been to a Knicks game?"

"Hey, don't take it personally. I just haven't been. Not many of my friends in the City are into sports and I refuse to pay the ticket price for me to schlep to the Garden by myself."

"You've got to be kidding me, but whatever. We'll discuss your lack of culture later," Matt said to his own amusement. "Then, it's settled. You're staying the night. You can go back to the City after the game tomorrow night."

"I guess I can stay. My column isn't due yet," Reese said while wondering how he got to this point with high school god Matt Walker. "Do you think I will I be able to get a hotel room this late at night?"

Matt thought briefly about his ability to hide his new crush from the rest of the team. He could say Reese was a friend from high school, again. Matt rationalized, most of the guys on the squad loved his column anyway. They would be talking about the Orthodox Jew story all night long.

"Don't sweat it, you can crash with me. Everybody on the team gets his own suite when we travel. I'm sure it'll have two beds, a pullout, or a king, if you don't mind having to sleep with me," Matt said with his now-familiar devilish grin. Then continuing with his own elbow jab to Reese's torso and saying, "And, I'm sure that this won't be the first or last time you would sleep with a man."

"Easy enough. Oh wait! Shit! Logan!" Reese exclaimed as he thought of his poor dog being stuck at Taylor's apartment for another night.

"Oh, he your boyfriend?" he asked with visions of a perfect reunion crashing before him.

"No, he's my bulldog," Reese said while digging through his messenger bag for his cell phone. "My friend, Taylor, is watching him while I'm gone. It's not going be pleasant telling her she has to keep him another night."

"That's so cool. I had a chocolate lab in college. He was a great hit. I bet you get lots of attention walking him in the City."

"I've had him fetch me a boy or two in Central Park," Reese said as he found his phone under a wasteland of mints, condoms and pens. "If you'll excuse me, I better give my bitch a call before she cooks up my dog for a midnight snack."

Reese looked around the dark and silent cabin wondering, briefly, how everyone was managing to sleep upright on a train— a feat he had never been able to accomplish on any type of transport vehicle. When he stood up to exit the train car, his eyes caught the eyes of an elderly and apparently highly annoyed woman. He figured her proximity to his conversation with Matt had probably kept her awake. He gave her an apologetic look before heading towards the café car.

As Reese walked through the gently swaying train, trying his best not to jar anyone from their peaceful slumber, he gave a quick thought back to the agitated woman. A few years ago he would have been severely affected by her attempt at a guilt-inducing look. A concern for the opinions of others had been a curse imparted to him by his father. Luckily, the anonymity of the City was quickly eroding this bulkhead of self-consciousness. Reese shook off his thoughts and dialed Taylor on the cell phone.

"You better be in a taxi on your way over here to get this damn dog," Taylor answered on the other line of the phone.

"Hello to you, too. How's my baby? Are you two getting along any better?" Reese asked, trying to play coy and not be directly confrontational.

"I've about had it with this thing, Reese. It's so freaking gross, how do you deal with picking up his shit?"

"He's not a thing, and letting him hear you badmouth him is probably going to end up costing you," Reese pleaded. "I would watch your newest pair of Fendi mules. He might want to make another statement. But seriously, Logan just needs a little more time to get adjusted to new his surroundings. Another night and he'll love you forever."

"Don't even think about it. You are coming over here right now and reclaiming this beast."

"No can do babe. I'm staying the night in Philly," he said and paused for dramatic effect before continuing, "with Matt Walker."

"You're what?" Taylor shrieked. "Matt Walker? NBA Matt Walker? What are you doing with him?"

"Actually he's Mister NBA Matt Walker to you," he said in his most smart-ass tone. "He was at the ceremony and asked me to join him as his guest for tomorrow's game against the 76ers."

"Oh my God! I didn't know you two were friends."

"We're not. Not really, I guess. Hell, I don't know, Tay. We just hit it off and now we're on a train to Philadelphia."

"You damn fags move so fast," she cracked as Reese could see her smirk from 200 miles away.

"No, that's not it at all. He's straight. Why does everyone think he's gay?" Reese asked rhetorically. "But he's letting me stay with him tonight. I can't be an ass and turn all that down. Maybe it'll even give me something to write about for next week's column. You can handle Logan for one more night. Just take him for a few walks, let him drink from the toilet and bring an extra blanket to bed so he can nuzzle you without stealing the covers."

"You're going to owe me so much Reese Gibbons. I'm talking big time . . . like getting me a date with your hot new straight friend. Anyway, have fun babe, get him drunk and maybe you'll really have something to write about in your column."

Chapter Five

Making their way through the front door of the Ritz-Carlton in downtown Philadelphia with their bags was nearly impossible due to the rush of bellmen standing at attention in their neat red jackets and white pants. "It looks like they're off to a fox hunt," Reese said as they walked through the hotel's grand Rotunda lobby with its stark white marble Doric columns and opulent oriental rugs.

As Matt checked in with the front desk, Reese felt as if he was walking into a lion's den of straightness. Numerous coaches and players meandered through the lobby, noting Matt's arrival with a wave or hello before moving onto their night's destination.

"Is there a couch or a second bed in my suite?" Matt asked the attractive blond front desk girl, after flashing his Knicks travel ID.

"There is a sofa bed that can be pulled out," she said with a touch of a smile lingering around her mouth. "We can have that made up for you, if you would like."

Matt agreed and had the bellman take the bags up to his suite. "Why don't we check out the bar and see if anyone is around," he suggested to Reese as the two stood admiring the domed ceiling and lavishly decorated walls.

"It's after one in the morning. Won't it be closed?" Reese asked, hoping that the night would end and he could get some rest.

"Welcome to the NBA," Matt said with a wink of his left eye. "Hotels keep their bars and restaurants open when they have a visiting team to accommodate our later schedule. You're not tired, are you?" he asked, sort of hoping that Reese wanted to retire for the evening, but quickly remembering that it would raise more suspicions if they just ran up to his room.

"Not really. It could just be the beers taking effect."

"You only had a few," Matt said with disgust. "Let's get the party started again, so I can get something to eat."

Heading through the lobby to the hotel's Pantheon bar where jazz filled the candlelit room Matt noticed a few more players including his closest friend on the team, Wayne Hawkins. Wayne was sitting in the back corner, eating a sandwich and drinking his signature Lemon Lime Gatorade.

"Did you just get in?" Matt asked his friend.

"About an hour ago," Wayne answered while ingesting a Philly cheese steak and a baked potato. "Who's your friend?"

"Oh, sorry man. This is Reese Gibbons," Matt said as his travel companion offered his hand. "He went to high school with me and was traveling back to the City before I got him to join us for the game tomorrow."

"Don't you work for the *Voice*?" Wayne asked.

"I write a column," Reese answered.

"You did that piece on the East Village slut and her Ortho-Jew boyfriend. That cracked my shit up."

"I heard it was a hit with the team," Reese laughed with an uneasy smile.

"Would love to stay and talk but Anthony challenged me to a game," Wayne said as he wiped his plate with the crust of his sandwich. "It's going off in Twan's room in five. You wanna join us?"

"A game this late?" Reese inquired.

"On PlayStation2," Wayne answered. "We all have created teams comprised entirely of ourselves on NBA Live and we play each other over and over again."

"Surprisingly, this is how the guys in the League spend their time," Matt informed Reese. "The only problem is that the boys who designed the game, make judgments on everyone's skills. I mean, they made Wayne here a ball-handling god."

"Don't get pissy with me, Casper," Wayne retorted. "It's not my fault that the boys at EA Sports gave you no handles."

Wayne quickly finished up and exited the now-deserted restaurant. "Wayne seems like a nice guy," Reese offered as the waiter came with a salad for Reese and a grilled chicken breast for Matt.

"Aw, Wayne is the man," Matt said as he dug into his garlic-mashed potatoes. "Considering what a raw deal he got in college, he's making the most of his opportunity in the League."

As Matt explained it, Wayne was the ringleader of the Knicks, on and off the court. With his heady playmaking ability and deadly outside shot, the Atlanta native was considered one of the League's top point guards. He was growing fond of playing alongside his good friend in the backcourt when Matt would replace the usual starter, Anthony Michaels.

Matt noted the irony in that the two were fast friends considering the contrast of their backgrounds. Like Matt, Wayne had been an All-American in college, but the duo's legacies could not have been more different. While Matt's number hung in the rafters in Palo Alto, Wayne's jersey has been removed from its former home at the University of Georgia.

Considered a hoops God since the age of thirteen, Wayne was the biggest prospect to come out of the South in nearly a decade. He honed his lightning-quick feet and silky smooth passes in Atlanta's poverty-ridden neighborhoods. The combination of hard work and abundant talent made him one of the few point guards, not from New York City, to be considered good enough to jump directly to the NBA from high school.

But to his mother's satisfaction and father's dissatisfaction, Wayne decided to play for the Georgia Bulldogs before venturing on to the professional level. Wayne earned instant stardom by leading the NCAA in scoring and assists in his first two years in Athens. After announcing he would be leaving school for the League after his third year with a degree, *Sports Illustrated* ran a cover story with Wayne's father admitting to have accepted over half a million dollars for funneling his son to the University of Georgia.

While Wayne never saw a dime of his father's deal, the NCAA immediately suspended the two-time All-American and placed the athletic program on probation for five years, nearly giving it the death penalty.

A severe public backlash against Wayne ensued, resulting in his banishment from the Bulldog family. Although considered the best basketball player to ever dress in a Georgia uniform, Wayne is not listed as a letterman or contributor to Georgia's program in any way.

Now in his eighth year as a professional for the New York Knicks, Wayne was a two-time All Star and making a name for himself away from his father's tragic actions. He was leading the League in assists and had the lowest number of turnovers for a starting point guard.

When Matt finished his dessert of chocolate ice cream and raspberries, he suggested that the two meet up with the other players in Twan's room, as he believed they would be playing deep into the morning as they usually did.

"What are these guys going to be like?" Reese asked as he fought back a yawn in the elevator up to the fourteenth floor.

Entering the suite of the Knick power forward Antoine Daniels, Matt and Reese found the room occupied by Wayne and two other guys. Huddled around the Playstation2, Wayne battled a young man who looked no more than twenty years old, while the third was on his cell phone in the back of the room.

Reese tried to knock out his feeling of discomfort as he and Matt sat on a sofa adjacent to the video game activity. A blue team was pounding a team in white and red.

"Anthony," Wayne cried out. "If you don't stop hacking me, I'm going to turn the fouls back on."

"That's shit," Anthony sassed as he smacked the back of Wayne's head. "Don't even think that you're going to get in the lane old man."

"Boy, don't even go there," Wayne warned. "If you were

actually this good, Matt wouldn't be stealing your minutes on the court."

Slamming down his game controller, Anthony launched into a tirade with many phrases and words Reese couldn't follow. Finally, Anthony, looking coldly at Matt, exclaimed, "Fuckin' white bread ain't gonna take my game."

As the door slammed behind the departing Anthony, a larger black man in the back of the room asked, "Handles, what did you say to Kid?"

"Nothin'," Wayne mumbled.

"Kid can't handle the truth," the man in the back said while looking at Reese.

"He told him that he isn't as good as he is on the game," Matt interjected.

"Jesus Christ," the man said as he walked over and picked up Anthony's abandoned controller and began finishing the game versus Wayne. "Every fucking time you start loosing to Kid, you have to bring up that he has skills on PS2, but not on the court. Damn, rookie move, Wayne."

"It's not my fault those geeks at EA Sports made him look like Mike," Wayne pleaded, "and God knows he ain't the Answer or Kobe either."

"You just do that 'cause he beats the crap out of you," the man said before turning to Reese. "Now, who are you?"

"I'm Reese, a friend of Matt's from high school."

"He's the writer from the *Voice*," Wayne interjected.

"Aww, shit," he exclaimed. "Did you write that crap about my girl and her Jew sugar daddy?"

"Was that required reading?" Reese asked in utter disbelief that his column had not only reached professional athletes but had been retained.

"It should have been," he answered. "I'm Antoine Daniels, but call me Twan."

Twan's attention turned back to his game versus Wayne. Since taking over Anthony's team the lead had grown from eight to twenty-two points in a matter of moments. Later in the evening

Reese was taught how to play and was allowed to play as the never-used all-Michael Jordan team. He never lost by less than fifty points as the four men continued to talk and play their virtual selves until sunrise.

*　*　*

"Housekeeping," came muffled from the other side of the double door to Matt's suite, which had been knocked upon for the past minute.

Reese stumbled to his feet from the pullout sofa bed where he laid his head last night. "Matt, do you need anything?" he asked before noticing Matt's bed lay empty and he was nowhere to be found.

"I don't think we need anything, thank you," Reese told the housekeeper after cracking the door the necessary three inches it was required to see the tiny Latino woman and be polite, yet not enough for her to see his morning wood poking at his boxer briefs.

Finding a note on the floor on his way to the bags placed neatly by the suite's round dining table, Reese read, "Didn't want to wake you. Gone to the shoot around. I'll be back around two. Be ready to roll."

It was a quarter after one already.

As the sun filled every inch of the extravagantly decorated room, Reese couldn't believe that he slept as long as he did. Yet he couldn't believe that he started the night at a banquet for his high school and ended up playing video games with the New York Knicks.

"What a fuckin' weird night," he said to himself while grabbing his toothbrush and toothpaste.

He needed a shave and a shower, a call to check in with Taylor as well as one to his editor. He knew that he wouldn't be able to get his copy in by its usual Saturday night deadline, but he also knew they really didn't need it before Sunday night or Monday morning at the latest.

Finding his cell phone on its last bar of juice, Reese contemplated getting in one call to his editor before it went dead. He decided to use that precious bar of energy for Taylor and not his editor, so he picked up the suite's phone and dialed his long distance carrier in hopes of billing it back to the *Voice*.

"David, it's Reese," he said as the call went directly to voicemail. "I'm in Philadelphia for the Knicks game tonight. My copy is going to be a tad late, but fret not; I'll have it to you first thing tomorrow. If you have a problem with it, kiss my ass. No seriously, David, kiss my ass. Talk to you soon."

David had been Reese's editor for years, and they were always very playful with each other. He had first recruited Reese to the *Voice* when the promising young writer was in a Mass Media and Diversity class David was teaching at NYU. To David, Reese had a marvelous ability to capture the heart of an obscure issue while putting a mainstream twist upon it, making it easier for his audience.

*   *   *

Situated across Penn Square from the Ritz Carlton rose Philadelphia's 510-foot tall City Hall, which pierced the skyline at the exact geographical center of William Penn's original city plan. Its huge granite mass continues to be one of the nation's finest examples of French Second-Empire Architecture. While controversy had surrounded the building from its earliest conception in 1860, it had weathered the storm of criticism of local politics, budgetary constraints to maintain it and campaigns to demolish the nearly 150-year-old structure. It was a standing testament to perseverance and resolve under pressure as it earned a great deal of respect for its unique achievement.

"The fact that a building, no less the City Hall, in a city with a history like Philadelphia is done in such an architecturally opulent Baroque style is one of the more amazing aspects of the building," Matt said while looking directly at Reese in an attempt to solicit some sort of response.

"Um, OK," Reese responded obviously lost and confused.

Surprised, yet delighted, by Reese's lack of knowledge on the subject, Matt continued, "Wow, you really meant that what you liked about the Chrysler building is that it's big and shiny."

Reese easily detected Matt's successful attempt at mocking sarcasm and responded with his own personal sarcastic style. Reese gave him the finger as they walked through City Hall's front doors.

"Oh, Mister *Village Voice* columnist is out of his league when the conversation ventures away from Power Puff Girls, Orthodox married men and their stripper whores or just being gay," Matt said, ribbing the fellow tourist.

As a security guard was quickly approaching them, Matt attempted to usher Reese away into the East Portal. "Welcome back, Mister Walker," she said. "Did you forget something from this morning?"

"You were here this morning?" Reese asked with a smile plastered from ear to ear.

"No ma'am," he answered the usher. "I just wanted to show my friend what I learned. Thank you for all your help."

Turning to Reese, he conceded, "Fine. You caught me."

"But why?"

"Well, I thought I would look stupid if I didn't do my homework. I figured I built my knowledge of architecture too much last night on the train."

"You didn't have to come early. We could have learned about it together."

"It's just my nature. Study and work harder than everyone else and you *might* be good enough. Don't let your weaknesses show."

"We're not on a basketball court," Reese offered. "It's fine if you don't know everything. Hell, I hardly know anything yet I pull a column out of my ass every week."

Matt smiled as the two meandered through the timeless building, looking at its hundreds of sculptures and various meeting rooms. Matt continued to tell Reese what he had learned just hours before, but in a less authoritative and more humble manner.

"Can I ask you a question?" Reese ventured while the two strolled through the center courtyard on a particularly warm March afternoon.

"Sure."

"Now, don't take this the wrong way," Reese said meekly. "But when we were hanging out last night with Twan and Wayne, I noticed that your voice had gotten deeper than when it was just the two of us on the train."

"What are you talking about?" he asked while looking up, trying to examine the pitch of the south side's roofline. "My voice doesn't change."

"Your voice on the train was like it is now, light and cheerful."

"Light and cheerful," Matt mocked with a singsong tone.

"Yes," Reese confirmed. "But, last night it was deeper and more monotone."

"I honestly don't know what you're talking about," Matt lied. "It could have been the alcohol or just getting tired."

"You're probably right. Or, I could have been hallucinating."

As his last words still hung in the air, Reese's nearly dead cell phone rang. Noticing it was his editor, David, he quickly directed the call to his voicemail. "I don't want to talk to him right now."

"Who was that? Your boyfriend?" Matt asked in another state of panic.

"Thank God, no." Reese said, fighting back his laughter. "It was my forty-eight-year-old editor. I called him this morning to say my copy would be late. It's no big deal."

"Well, that's good. I wouldn't want you to worry about that while you're at the game tonight. But while we're on the subject, do you have a boyfriend?"

"Nope."

"Why not?"

"I just broke up with a guy who I had dated for about a year on New Year's Eve," Reese said matter-of-factly.

"What happened?"

"What do you mean?"

"I'm just wondering that if you broke up on New Year's Eve, there must be a story behind it," Matt argued.

"There's a story behind every breakup."

"Why are you being so evasive?"

"I'm not. It's just not that important," Reese conceded before finally continuing as Matt looked into his eyes for an answer. "We broke up because we had different views on how a relationship worked. He thought it was all right to sleep with half of Chelsea and I thought it wasn't."

"So you found out about him that night?"

"I caught him that night," Reese said, turning more solemn as they approached the front of the hotel. "We were at a party at my friend's loft in Tribeca. It's a great space, really. High thirty-foot ceilings, huge windows and all very open."

"A bit too open?"

"For Adam, yes. I arrived late because I had to attend some early evening get together for the *Voice*. When I got there, he was already tweaking from his party drug of choice and eating the ass of a random boy from Jersey in the lofted bed space, which overlooked the apartment from fifteen feet."

"In front of everyone?"

"Not really. I think only the host and myself knew. Adam was sly and didn't let anyone else see. Of course, as soon as I saw, it became a huge drama."

"I'm sorry," Matt offered. "Was that the only time he did that?"

"He had been with other guys early in our relationship, but said he stopped after we became more serious. But I learned that he never did stop after more friends told me about his adventures after we split."

"Nice friends to tell you after the fact."

"I think they thought that Adam and I had set boundaries for each of us to play around," Reese reasoned. "But we didn't, because I didn't want to live like that. To me a relationship shouldn't have limitations. I wouldn't want to have a relationship that's defined by a contract of what actions are in play and which are out of bounds. But contract or no contract, Adam kept stepping out of bounds."

Chapter Six

As Reese settled into his seat to watch his first professional basketball game, he felt quite out of place. Not ever being much of a sports fan—Reese had never felt the urge to engage in the stereotypical young American male activities that included begging one's dad to take you to a professional sporting event or even attending after-school competitions—Reese's discomfort was also agitated by his memories of always being picked last for teams because of his thinness and overall horrible hand-eye coordination.

"Hi, you must be Reese," said an approaching young man in his mid-twenties. "I'm Heath Fletcher, Matt's roommate in New York."

"Hey . . . Hi," Reese answered awkwardly.

"Yeah, I knew it was you. I've seen your picture in the *Voice*," Heath continued as he settled into the seat beside Reese. "I just took the train down to see the game. You're on your way back to the City?"

"Yeah, the train was my only option last night and then Matt offered a ticket to the game, so I decided to stop over."

"Yeah, he made me drop Alex from today's plans so you could have this ticket. Last night was our second date, so God knows the pay off would have come today with a day trip to Philly for a Knicks game."

"Oh," Reese said as his jaw continued descending to the floor. He could not believe Heath was open about his latest trick in what Reese perceived as the church of straightness—the athletic arena. "Maybe," he thought, "Matt collects young gay men for friends and this side trip into Philly was his recruitment of me."

"Yeah, Alex is my latest piece of ass. What about you? You seeing anyone?" Heath continued.

"No, not really."

Standing nearly six feet tall and solidly built with a light brown curly shag atop his head, Heath was nearly as attractive as Matt. Reese's mind wandered as he considered how hot the two roommates were and wished Bel Ami Studios would be so lucky to have the two boys duke it out over or under the sheets. What delicious possibilities, Reese thought.

"Well, that's good," Heath said while slapping the back of the man in front of Reese. "Kevin! What's going on with my favorite beat writer?"

"Hello, Heath," Kevin said in dramatic, yet monotone fashion. "I was wondering who was behind me talking about ass."

"Kevin, let me introduce you to a fellow scribe," Heath said, nodding toward Reese. "This is Reese Gibbons. He actually writes about things you wouldn't understand. You know, for the *Voice*."

"If it's in the *Voice*, then no one understands it," Kevin said while shaking Reese's hand. "Kevin Ashby, nice to meet you. I cover the Knicks for the *Post*."

"Shouldn't you be in a press area?" Reese asked.

"Nah, Kevin's too cool for school," Heath said. "He likes it up here, with all us common folk."

"I don't like press row," Kevin replied. "It's all about the agents and League publicists down there. Up here, I get the real story. Actually, I could file my stories from watching the game on the television. I would just need the post-game quotes."

"Kevin, you are the life of the party," Heath chimed in. "I think I met someone who would be perfect for you. She is just about your speed. Of course, I discovered her last week when I was visiting my grandmother at a nursing home. But she flat lined before I left. I think she was nearly ninety-seven years old. It was a shame. She was a looker, too."

With Heath's last jibe at the nerdy beat writer, the three settled into their seats for the start of the game. Heath served up a play-by-play for Reese and tried to give him as much insight into the game as he could. But it was obvious, when Heath mentioned the tension between Matt and Anthony Michaels, that he was keeping his voice low enough so Kevin could not hear it.

"See, Matt was drafted by the Knicks to push Anthony to play better," Heath whispered. "Anthony was picked right out of high school a year before Matt was drafted and quickly became an all-star on the hype. But Anthony doesn't show up to play every night. The kid is loaded with cash, yet his attitude sucks. Matt thinks it's drugs, but who knows for sure? In the past month, Matt's playing time has increased and he will probably start, if Anthony doesn't clean his act up. If Matt does start, it's worth millions to him. See, Matt's first contract is up at the end of the season and he becomes a free agent. This is the chance Matt's been waiting for his entire life."

Reese attempted to take it all in, but was distracted by the grace with which Matt moved up and down the court. He accumulated eight points in the first half and started the second half.

"See I told you," Heath exclaimed. "This is it. The coaches are sick of Anthony. It's Matt's position now."

As the game concluded, Heath led Reese downstairs to the visiting locker room and the victorious Knicks. Matt had scored twenty-six points while dishing seven assists. He was named the game's MVP.

Matt was shirtless with a towel around his waist standing at his locker surrounded by cameramen and reporters when Heath and Reese walked into the locker room. Trying not to stare was getting harder and harder to accomplish as Reese noticed that Matt's perfectly smooth chest was still glistening from his shower. Matt's broad shoulders were also a prize for Reese's eyes to feast upon. His gaze ventured south to Matt's rippled arms and damp abdominals peppered with fine golden hair.

"Hey, guys!" Matt shouted to his visiting duo from across the locker room once the media entourage departed for a dejected Anthony in the far corner. Matt considered throwing on a shirt, but decided to allow his chest to do some nonverbal flirting for him.

"Big man!" Heath exclaimed running over to Matt and clasping hands and patting him on the back. "You rocked out there. What was with your pull-up fifteen-footer over Iverson in the third quarter? You know that was total shit. And shit, that's my game."

"I learned from the best," Matt conceded before looking over to Reese. "How did you like the game? I told you it would be a good time. I hope this fool didn't bore you to death."

"Not at all," Reese said. "Heath was a great resource for my first professional basketball game."

"When is the last train to get back to the City?" Matt asked.

"I think it's in an hour or two," Reese offered.

"Ninety minutes," Heath concluded.

"Excellent, so you two can help me celebrate for a while," Matt said while nodding to a few of the other players as they departed the locker room. "The other players are taking off to a strip club, but that isn't my scene."

"Oh come on, big dog," Heath joked. "You don't want to go join the pack and hunt the beaver?"

"Not this time," Matt said sheepishly. "Plus, I don't think Reese would be too comfortable there."

"Don't let me change your plans. You said you would show me the life of a real NBA player, and if that's in a strip joint in Philadelphia with snatch staring me in the face, so be it."

"Reese, don't worry," Heath said with a big grin on his face. "I think you would be more comfortable looking at cooter than Matt would be. He's never been a big fan." Matt shot his roommate the look of death, and Heath quickly shut his mouth tilting his head away, pissed that he had said something so obvious.

As the locker room was nearly deserted, the trio departed for the team's hotel to have a few rounds at the trendy lobby bar. As the three young men walked through the player's entrance there were nearly two hundred people waiting to gain a photo or a word with the newest star of the NBA.

"Go ahead and get in the car," Matt said. "I'm just going to sign a few autographs if I see any kids along the rail."

"You're such a Saint," Heath quipped as he grabbed Reese's arm to lead the backstage virgin into the waiting black limousine.

The trio quickly departed and headed off to the team's hotel in downtown Philadelphia.

Drifting into the hotel was not as simple as it was the night before. Nearly thirty people clogged the lobby trolling for autographs. The coaches and a few of the reserves stopped and talked with the fans once again.

"They're here to see the star," Heath exclaimed while nudging Matt through the front door.

"There he is!" exclaimed a young woman in her early twenties as she spotted Matt entering the lobby. As a swarm of young women flocked to their latest heartthrob, Reese and Heath fell to the side and waited for the elevator.

Once the doors closed and they began ascending to the fourteenth floor, Heath said, "The boy is too good looking not to explode. Being a starter on the team in the largest media market is huge. And let's not forget the simple fact that the NBA will market the hell out of him since he's white. He's going to be the NBA's answer to the NFL's Jason Sehorn, a marketable white athlete that you can sell to the family in Iowa."

"Wasn't this just one game?" Reese asked.

"Tonight was the culmination of the season's event," he said while opening the suite door. "You were just lucky enough to witness it."

It took Matt nearly twenty minutes to reach his suite, and Heath was ready to call for a cab after downing a quick drink from the bar. "Dude, we got to be going. The train is in less than thirty minutes. You know I would stay, but I have to prep for the European Union's policy meetings for the bank tomorrow."

"You both can't leave," Matt pleaded. "Reese, you don't have to prep for whatever Heath just said. Do you?"

"My editor is expecting my latest column," Reese answered with disappointment ringing loud and clear.

"Do you have to hand it in?"

"No, e-mail."

"Then you're staying here and writing it tomorrow," Matt said, not believing his own nerve.

"I don't have a say in this?"

"Apparently, not," Heath answered. "Well, man, congratulations on a great game. Call me tomorrow from Miami when your coach names you starter. I gotta roll." Nodding towards Reese, "Very nice to meet you. I hope this boy treats you well tonight."

Heath got in one quick wink of his left eye to his roommate, then as quickly as he appeared next to Reese in the arena earlier that evening, he disappeared through the suite's double doors.

Attempting to keep the conversation from dying off and making Matt regret his decision to recruit Reese as a wingman for the evening, the young columnist turned to the young basketball professional and inquired, "So do you really think you're going to start in Miami?"

"That's up to the coach to decide," he said as if he was sidestepping the latest political scandal. "Want a drink?"

"Of course."

"The bar is over there," Matt said with his patented devilish grin.

"Wow, back-to-back MVP performances and the Diva comes out," Reese said while pouring two highballs with Maker's Mark and Ginger Ale. "Well, here is the only 'breeder' couple I like— Mark and Ginger. No offense."

"None taken," Matt said when taking the glass from Reese.

The duo quickly fell into conversation far from the world of basketball and White Hall Academy and their City Hall excursion. As the bourbon continued to flow the two slid closer together, then Reese noticed Matt's touch of his hand when passing along his third drink of the night. At first Reese thought nothing of it and chalked it up to a set of growing drunken inhibitions. But when Matt's fingers began to grasp for Reese's hand and not the fresh glass of Mark and Ginger on the fourth and fifth round, Reese realized with a start that Matt was not doing anything accidentally.

The past forty-eight hours rushed through Reese's mind. The whole weekend was Matt's idea from offering the car to the train station where the two could travel together to the near guilt trip into staying in Philadelphia for a game the next day. Matt had been helpful and polite and courteous. Was everyone right? Was Matt Walker gay and was he now making a move for Reese? But, how did Heath play into this?

"Heath's a great guy," Reese tentatively offered. "How did you two meet?"

"We were at Stanford together. He was a walk-on with the basketball team. We roomed together on the road and he's now an analyst for Smith Barney."

"Roomed together, huh? That must have been fun," Reese said with a sinful grin.

Not noticing the sexual overtone, Matt continued, "It was OK. He snores out of his mind. I can't imagine how all the girls put up with him."

"Oh, he dates girls?"

"Yeah, a lot of them. He was listed last year in the *New Yorker* as one of Manhattan's top young bachelors. Actually, we both were. Did you think he was gay?"

"I guess I did. With the exception of his sports knowledge, he was setting off my gaydar—especially when he spoke of Alex."

"*Alexandra* is our neighbor. She models for J. Crew and those other places where all the girls look like twigs and have no pores. He's been trying to bag her for about seven months," Matt said. Continuing with more than mockery in his voice, "and, just because someone knows about sports doesn't mean that they aren't gay, Reese."

"I know. I'm just being obtuse. I mean my people are quite proficient in their sports knowledge. In fact most of my friends can talk for hours of their own ab workouts or the latest developments in the worlds of figure skating, gymnastics and diving."

"For being such an open-minded person, you can be quite a smart ass. Now, not to be too forward thinking, but gay men are some of our biggest fans."

"Well, I think you gained another one tonight," Reese said with a wide smile.

"Then I hope you will join me for future games, and in the post-game celebrations to come as well." Matt said as he pinned Reese against the edge of the suite's sofa in which the pair had been sitting. Reese's mouth dropped open, but Matt couldn't take it anymore. He had to show Reese he wanted it too. He was sure of it, now more than ever.

With no hesitation, Matt landed his full lips upon Reese's soft and open mouth. And as the two's tongues moved wildly about, their hands began to explore their bodies. Soon enough, Matt had unbuttoned Reese's latest purchase from Dolce & Gabana and had headed south along his body's light but distinct line of abdominal definition.

As Matt was working his right hand against Reese's crotch and unbuttoning his Diesel jeans with his left, Reese's mind swirled with bourbon and visions of their reunion. Finally, Reese succumbed to his conflicts and screamed, "What the fuck is going on? You were the captain of the basketball team and Prom King! Are you fucking with me dude?"

"Jesus, man! Haven't you noticed I've been trying to keep you around ever since I ran into you at school?" Matt responded as he continued to undress Reese. "I've wanted inside these pants since we sat down for dinner last night, and I may have gotten that blowjob at the train station but I don't think you've had a chance to get off since the weekend began." Matt trailed off as he lowered his head onto Reese's throbbing cock.

*   *   *

Sun light bathed the room as Reese awoke to a light snoring

and to the gentle comfort of Matt spooning him. Enjoying a few seconds of content before being bombarded with memories of the previous night, Reese's heart began to race as the spacious room and bed began to be too small for the two grown men waking up that morning.

While Reese welcomed last night's advances, he began to wonder what Matt's personality would be that morning. Was Matt gay? Or was he a sexual opportunist who saw Reese as his only option from last night? What was the protocol for a trick of a celebrity, or worse, a closeted male professional athlete? Would Matt wake to utter confusion from not being able to recall his drunken actions from hours before? Or would Matt know why he was naked in bed next to his high school yearbook editor with three used condoms on the bedside table?

Almost sensing Reese's deafening heartbeat, Matt jumped out of bed and bounded into the bathroom. Reese remained in bed, immobile from his own hangover, but mostly from his own fear.

All, or rather, most of Reese's questions were addressed to his relief when Matt came racing from the bathroom and dove naked under the covers, but on top of Reese.

"Good morning sexy, you sleep all right?"

"I slept great," Reese answered. "Maybe a bit of confusion set in this morning. I mean, how did we get here?"

A stunned Matt asked, "You don't remember last night?"

"Oh, I remember how we got here and what we did over there and there and there," Reese said while pointing to the points where the two lovers had slowly moved across the room from its lavish leather couch to the glass table and finally to the bed. "But I'm asking about *here*. I mean, you're Matt Walker, a star on the New York Knicks."

"Not really a star, but thanks for the confirmation of my employer," Matt said with more sarcasm and attitude Reese had heard outside of Chelsea in a long while. "And remember you're Reese Gibbons, *Voice* columnist. Now, that we've got our names straight—notably after the sex. Damn, I guess this *is* a gay date."

Stopping to think of whether Reese could see him as just Matt and not a professional athlete or the jock of his high school class was the first objective. He desperately wanted to say "stay and be with me—we can address the other issues later." But he couldn't find his voice. Finally, he just swallowed hard and feebly asked, "You're not one of those fags that freaks out the morning after are you?"

Taken aback Reese just smiled and answered, "No, I'm not going to freak out, as long as you don't." The two embraced and giving no pause to the other's rank morning breath, kissed long and deep. The pair did not come up for air until the fourth and final condom within Reese's messenger bag had been worked through.

Chapter Seven

Sitting in the cramped spare bedroom he called his den in his Hell's Kitchen apartment, Reese typed away on his laptop, trying to formulate some type of column for the week. Now an hour from his drop-dead deadline, the point where he could no longer submit his column, he had two 750-word columns completed.

Both columns had started out as attempts to write about his night with four members of the New York Knicks in a suite at the Philadelphia Ritz-Carlton. He found it fascinating that there were people in this world whose job was so fascinating that it was simulated on a video game and could be mimicked by anyone, even the people on whom the virtual characters are based.

He wondered what other games could be developed where someone could play himself. A policeman would be the most obvious, with its infinite possibilities from chasing down speeding cars to going on a SWAT raid. But most of the options he dreamed up had little-to-no sex appeal, like the accountant who has orders from his CEO to hide a billion dollars worth of losses. Of course to be declared a winner, you would work to keep your stock price high until you could exercise the options and retire to the tax-free Cayman Islands. There could be pesky Securities and Exchange Commission officials snooping around and there could be a speed round of paper shredding for bonus stock options.

Another game could be playing a social debutante where the goal was to get your name in the paper as many times as possible without having a real job or purpose. Certainly, the Hilton sisters would argue the game was based on their exploits; maybe they would want the endorsement deal. The commercial could be Nicky or Paris saying, "When I want to go out and party, I go out and party. But if the Concorde to Paris is booked, or I can't make it to a helicopter pad for a weekend in East Hampton, I stay at home and play 'The Hilton Sisters' on PlayStation2! Only on 'The Hilton Sisters' can you date rock stars, become a glorified extra in blockbuster movies and go topless in Times Square. Don't be Britney's back-up dancer. Be a Hilton Sister!"

As he tried to link his random thoughts, his column seemed to ramble on the page back to Matt, with his strong hands, warm eyes and soft lips. More than two days later Reese could still feel Matt's heavy breath on the back of his neck and his right arm draped around him as they lay in bed.

The two men, now lovers, had little time to discuss the implications of their actions. Matt had just minutes to leave with the team for a road game in Miami when the two came up for air late Sunday afternoon. They had spent the night and most of the day tangled up in each other and Reese wished it never had to end.

But it did, and he had found his way back to Manhattan and the numerous messages from his editor inquiring about this week's column, as well as Logan seeming to be afraid of any sudden movements.

"Did Taylor hurt you?" Reese asked his now timid dog while offering him another sausage treat in an attempt to coax him from under the den's futon where Logan would hide when he thought he had been bad. "I'll never leave you with her again. I promise."

As what Reese believed would be his final column attempt printed, a skittish Logan removed himself from his tomb with his favorite blanket draped from his clinched jaw. Logan placed his head upon his master's knee while Reese read the final column. When the high-pitched sound of Reese's cell phone went off, Logan jumped away and scurried under the futon.

Noticing the phone call was from Taylor, he rolled his eyes and wondered exactly what she did to his dog while he was away for the weekend. Logan only offered a slight whimper when Reese tried to get him to play or just emerge from his cavelike setting.

"What did you do to my damn dog?" he shouted into the phone.

"What?"

"Logan won't come out from under the futon, and he's whimpering all the time."

"I did nothing to your dog," she offered. "Nothing that he didn't do to himself."

"Spill it."

Taylor explained that after Logan's third assault on her precious shoe collection she finally yelled at him. "I never hit him, Reese. I promise. But he was skittish and when he was backing away, he turned to run after I throw a shoe close to him. But not at him! Well, when he turned, he ran right into my bookcase and it kinda fell on him."

"Oh my God," Reese said to his horror. "Was he hurt bad?"

"You should have seen it. I called an ambulance 'cause he was only walking on three legs," she said as she began to laugh. "But they said they wouldn't send one out for a dog. So I ended up wrapping him in a blanket and putting him in one of my duffle bags. He actually seemed to like it in there."

"Go on," Reese said trying not to think of the image of little Taylor stuffing his big dog in a duffle bag.

"Well, I couldn't carry him. Did you know he's sixty-five pounds?" she asked rhetorically. "So I tipped my doorman $200 to help me take him to the Animal Rescue Center on First Avenue. The vet said he was fine and gave him a shot for the pain. He was a perfect angel after that."

"I'm sure he was after you threw a bookcase at him," Reese said, milking the story for every drop it was worth.

"Look, you're not mad so stop it," she reasoned. "But God knows, you will remind me of it enough in the coming years to make sure I take care of the mutt again."

"I don't think I will ever let you keep him again," he said, knowing that he had just made a challenge. Taylor would now most certainly want to keep Logan when Reese was called away from New York.

"Get over it," she said. "I have a meeting in five minutes. Now, are we going to Pastis tonight or not?"

"Sure. My place at eight?"

"Done."

*　　*　　*

Opening his front door at a half past eight o'clock, Reese found Taylor dressed in a tight, low swinging number that trailed off around her waist and just above where her black pants hung off her small hips. Her stiletto-heeled shoes propped her frame up an additional three inches and were considered very necessary to keep her full-length coat from dragging the streets of Manhattan.

"Honey, you know I love you, but what is with this?" Reese said as he pointed at the latest addition to Taylor's wardrobe, which tried to bring attention to her mosquito-bite breasts.

"Don't start with me, fag," Taylor quipped while gathering a quick peck on her cheek and moving her way down Reese's long hallway to his comfortably decorated living room. Falling into his large, purple, velvet wingback chair, she continued, "I have to flaunt what God gave me."

"My breasts are larger than your baby nuggets."

"Yes, thanks to protein shakes and whatever else you get from GNC that will cause your dick to shrivel and fall off when you're forty," she snorted while digging through her unusually large trademark handbag. Others would use a bag of this size to pack for overnight trips, but with Taylor she contained her "life" within its leather veneer.

"But enough of how I spent three hundred dollars on this new top instead of the ten grand I chose not to spend upgrading my tits. If we don't get moving we're going to lose our table at Pastis, and there is no way in hell you're not treating me to several drinks and dinner after what your mutt did to half my favorite shoes."

Pulling what appeared to be clumps of intertwined leather snakes from her bag, Taylor made reference to her ruined collection of mules. "Since I have no use for these, I figure Logan might as well have them to play with and maybe work some of that grime off of his gnarly teeth."

"Bitch! He's got lovely, yet misaligned teeth. But you're right; I do owe you big time. Although, I'm going to stand strong and say the shoe mauling is your own fault for letting him think you don't like him. Be thankful you kept your bedside table's bottom drawer closed. I would have hated to see what he would have done to your vibrator."

Knowing where she kept her vibrator never embarrassed Reese; in fact, he loved the idea that he knew his friend's menstrual cycle and sexual routine. It always made those five days a month a little easier to take. "Anyways, knowing Benjie, he's already at the bar, waiting for us so he can be seated."

"I totally forgot Benjie was meeting us," she cried. "Now I don't feel rushed at all. That queen would go straight before letting someone skip over him on the reservation list. Realistically, he's probably slept with the host, or he at least knows him from the gym, so our spot is golden."

"So does this mean we get to take the subway?" Reese said, mimicking the enthusiasm of a ten-year-old at an amusement park with his usual "happy dance" of the cabbage patch arm cycle and bizarre leg kick straight from "Riverdance."

Taylor, at times quite the paradox, often played her part as an Upper East Side princess to a capital "U." While the consummate, young liberal detested Clarence Thomas, the Bushes and the FOX News Network, she was still the daughter of a conservative Senator from Mississippi. Her family upbringing was one that she had fought most of her life culminating with her denial to enroll at Vanderbilt or Ole Miss and then marry into the southern good ol' boy network. The decision to attend NYU in freethinking Manhattan was none other than a slap in her father's face.

But, Reese found great enjoyment in pointing out Taylor's

refusal to ride the subway—day or night. Her apparent snobbery did not stem from a concern for her personal safety; rather, her father's belief in the worst of "liberally run" New York. He had insisted if she was going to go to school there that she allow him to give her a taxi allowance. His instructions had ended with something like "no daughter of a U.S. Senator is going to ride in an underground train next to illegal immigrants, drunk crack whores and fairies dying from their plague."

The first couple of years in the City, Taylor rode the subway like any other New Yorker. She used her substantial taxi fund to supply Reese and herself with kitschy dorm art, drinks, cover charges to clubs, some occasional drugs, and plane fare to New Orleans for Mardi Gras.

All that changed when she moved into an apartment on the Upper East Side. She now traveled by taxi no matter how often Reese argued with her about it. Reese insisted that public transport was good for the City, and that, since he wrote for the people, he needed to spend as much time as possible with the rest of the commoners. So the fact that Taylor had agreed to a subway adventure was making Reese's night.

"Why do you always act like that?" asked an annoyed Taylor, mimicking his epileptic seizure of a dance movement in the middle of the 50th Street sidewalk. "You know I don't think I'm too good for it or something, I just don't see the point of waiting to be jammed in a giant sardine can when I can afford not to."

"I could afford not to as well, if Daddy sent me cab fare." Reese jabbed as he swiped his unlimited metro card through the turnstile.

"Ass! You know full well he doesn't send me that money since I graduated."

"Yeah but he helps pay the rent, so it balances out in the end."

"Like you're completely independent bitch," she countered, knowing full well that Reese's parents paid the nearly four hundred dollars a month for his health insurance.

"Oh I know I'm not, I was just trying to distract you so you didn't complain about how grimy the station was, and look, it worked, here comes the C train." A satisfied Reese beamed as he stepped back from the edge of the platform.

As they rode the train downtown, Reese noticed a disturbingly cute gay couple sitting at the other end of the train. He watched them as they held hands with their knees touching. One was whispering in the other's ear, making him chuckle and beam a wide smile. Reese imagined that the two men were very comfortable with each other and could spend most of weekends not speaking and easily handling the silence as they meandered through the *Sunday Times*. He wished that he could be that content with someone. He wondered if Matt could ever be that someone.

"You could at least not stare," Taylor said under her breath. "I mean I know it's been a while since Adam, but please don't think about getting into threesomes."

"What?" he said as the picture of Matt and himself in bed with Logan reading the City section quickly disappeared. "I was just thinking it'd be nice, you know?"

"Don't worry sweetie we'll find you someone nice and hung," she quipped as the C train came to a screeching halt at the 14th Street Station. "Anyways, let's get off this dirty thing."

Reese and Taylor ascended the steps in the direction of the trendy Meat Packing District nestled between lower Chelsea and the West Village along the Hudson River. A slight odor in the air, quite similar to the distinct smell of blood, permeated the region and reminded Reese of the less perverse, actual origin of the neighborhood's descriptive name.

After the pair entered the restaurant and asked the host about their table they were alerted to their friend's presence by having two Mojitos shoved into their hands by a tipsy Benjie Lucas.

"Where have you girls been? I got out of work, worked out, and still managed to get here and have three of these lovelies before you queens got here," Benjie said as he finished off what Reese hoped was the alleged third drink and not the fourth. "What? Did the missus have to put on her face?"

"No, it's not my fault," Taylor said while knowing a fag hag should always be seen, but only on the fag's schedule. She understood all too well that it was quite unacceptable for the men of her life to wait for her. "Reese insisted on taking the subway. And you look like you put far more time into getting ready than I did anyways."

"Oh honey, you look fabulous! I was talking about him, the real girl in this group!" Benjie exclaimed while offering his cheek to Taylor. "And thank you. I just got this whole ensemble last weekend at Barney's. I had to get something for this occasion. It's been two weeks! But don't you love how this sweater shows off my arms? Raphael, my trainer, made me blast them three times this week. What an evil whore. I was even too tired yesterday to get my usual facial at Nickel."

"Of course you beat us here, you live three blocks away," Reese said in an attempt to defend himself. But it made no difference as Benjie had moved on to another topic.

"Honeys, let me tell you, I haven't needed drinks this badly since I was dumped by that actor who will remain nameless to us forever," Benjie said as he waved down the host to indicate that they were ready for their table, "I am in the middle of some major drama."

Drama was Benjie's life. Being a producer for NBC's *Today*, he was living the fabulous life from hobnobbing with celebrities to the infinite rambling of his social calendar. He believed that dating was a waste of time and he would trade in a relationship for the "right" share on Fire Island.

"Oh Lord, what's going on now Benjie?" Taylor inquired as she followed the host to their table by a window so her boys could be in view of the Ken dolls walking past on the sidewalk, as well as the ones peppered through the dinning room.

"This fag didn't tell you?" he asked, shooting Reese a look of disbelief. "This is so Benjie."

"No, it seems he hasn't," began Taylor as she waited impatiently for the two men to decide who got to face which direction. "The only thing this one has been talking about is how much cooler he is now that he's friends with an NBA star."

"To you, too? Always so self-absorbed," laughed Benjie as he explained to Taylor that his landlord had recently forced him out of his apartment.

"How the hell did that happen, isn't your place rent controlled? I thought that they can't kick you out of rent controlled places," Taylor countered.

"According to my landlord, the lease doesn't say that it's rent controlled," Benjie explained, giving a history of his agitated relationship with the seventy-five-year-old man who owned his building. "Remember when the market went soft and I asked him to lower my rent?"

"Weren't you there for four months when you asked?" Taylor interjected.

"Honey, I was over market and he knew it," he continued. "But anyway, he never liked me after that. Well, when I asked for my new lease, so I could renew, he said that he didn't have to resign me as a tenant, which I still believe is against the law. But, to make a long story short . . ."

"Too Late!" shouted a bored Reese.

"Ha! Ha!" Benjie laughed sarcastically after taking a rather large sip of his drink. "It's your fault for not telling her already. Anyways, three more days until I'm out and on the street because I still haven't found a new place."

"Are you using a broker? That's how I found my place," Taylor asked as she raised her glass into the waiter's line-of-sight to indicate her need for another.

"Of course. Oh my God, that's been the one positive aspect of this whole fiasco. I have discovered why people in this city go apartment hunting for fun."

"I don't even wanna know where this is going," Reese said.

"It's the perfect way to get ideas for your apartment," Benjie shrieked to his own enjoyment. "Hell, even your wardrobe can be touched up."

"Your wardrobe?" Taylor inquired having been fully drawn into the spectacle that was Benjie.

"It was hysterical. I was looking at this apartment today . . .

one I actually might take if they redo the bathroom. So I'm walking around, checking out the bedroom, and I see this fabulous shirt draped on the desk chair. I wanted to know where it was from, so I picked it up and fiddled with the collar to look at the tag. The next thing I know, I hear the stunned broker freaking out and attempting to usher me out of the apartment before I can check out all the designers hanging in that huge walk-in closet of his. That would have been fun."

"He saw you? You're crazy," Reese said, rolling his eyes in utter disbelief.

"I just told him I liked the shirt. He gave me an odd look, and that was all. I'm sure people have done weirder things in this city."

After the three caught their breath from the latest adventure of Benjie's life, they decided that they had better peruse the menu before they ended up facedown on the cobbled streets outside the restaurant. The rest of the night was filled with more absurd stories from Benjie, interjected with occasional political debates stemming from Benjie's Log Cabin Republican agenda and his antagonistic approach to Taylor's own beliefs.

"I'm sorry Benjie," she said while contemplating her fourth drink of the evening. "My father would love your vote, but he couldn't care less if you were tied to a fence post in Wyoming and beaten to death. How could you support someone who wouldn't support you?"

Before Benjie could slur his response, Reese's luck changed with his cell phone vibrating in his jeans' right hip pocket. Reaching into his pocket, and checking the display, Reese quickly excused himself from the table.

"Sorry guys, gotta take this call. I'll be back."

"Who is it?" Benjie asked to a quickly departed Reese.

"What was that about?" he turned to ask Taylor.

"Who knows? He's been scurrying off on that phone for the past couple of days," she answered with a roll of her eyes in an attempt at looking clueless. But the alcohol raging through her petite frame made her appear more slushy and rolled out than responsive to Benjie's question. "He said something about his editor or a possible book deal. But, I think he's up to something. I wonder if that little slut is thinking about doing anything 'surprising' for my birthday. I'm going to kill him."

"I totally forgot. It's in like two weeks, right?"

As Benjie and Taylor settled into their latest round of mojitos, they continued on with their usual banter resulting in Benjie's attempt to acquire the latest line of Clinique products Taylor was marketing. Finally the duo noted Reese had made his way out of the crowded restaurant to the sidewalk they overlooked.

"Hey, what's up? You guys win?" Reese asked as he finally got his ear piece in straight so his hands wouldn't be susceptible to the rain-soaked chill of the night.

"Of course we won! But, not much else is going on. I just got back to the hotel," replied an obviously tired yet enthusiastic Matt.

"Then why aren't you with the guys checking out some snatch?"

"Fuck! I didn't even think about that. I wonder why? Oh yeah, cause I'd rather be checking you out."

"Uh huh. Sure you would. You probably say that to all the fans." Reese said, smiling so much he was sure the oncoming headlights from a taxi would be reflected from his freshly polished teeth gaping forth from his wide smile.

"Well, yeah, but just the special fans."

"And just how many of those are there, one in every port?" Reese asked with a nervous laugh, hoping it would be perceived as only a joke and not the invasion it actually was.

"Life on the road is lonely. It happens sometimes," Matt said matter-of-factly.

But with only dead air at the other end of the connection, Matt offered sheepishly, "Um, it was a joke."

"I know. I just tried to freak you out," Reese said in a not so convincing manner.

"Anyways, I just wanted to call and say 'Hey.' I wish you were here to help me celebrate, if you know what I mean."

"Oh I know. You're back in the City soon, right?"

"Yeah, one more road game," he offered. "It's in two days versus the Pacers. Should be a good one. Hopefully we'll have a four-game winning streak when we come back to the City."

"Awesome. Well, good luck. Glad you called. Give me a buzz when you're back in the City. Maybe we could go check out the Chrysler Building."

"There are lots of things we can check out. Maybe I'll give you a call tomorrow after practice. All right, gotta go, someone's at the door, it's probably room service. Talk to you soon."

"Bye!" Reese said as he heard the sound of the disconnection.

Standing there, head tilted back, looking up at New York's starless sky, Reese's wondered how long people can truly live in a place where the only stars are seen on Broadway and not in the sky above it. But then his mind turned to what it had been on since he left the Ritz-Carlton in Philadelphia. How much energy should he invest in this newfound relationship? Was it a relationship at all? Was he a trick? A whore? Or was he more? Was there a boy in every port? Was Reese one of many, or few, or the only one? And if he was the only one, how could Matt not be dating someone else? He was numbingly handsome, well spoken, educated, intelligent, and an overall pleasant person. Everyone in New York probably wanted to date Matt.

"Shit!" Reese said out loud. He thought most straight guys in New York would probably date Matt if he offered.

If Matt was dating anyone, Reese thought, there was no way that no one would know about it. The informants for the New York Press's gossip pages, as well as the nefarious rumormongers making their living on the Internet, were more effective than the Third Reich's SA officers. Reese even thought back to his own research for his column on the secret gay loves of some of the country's most famous actors, athletes and politicians. He had found evidence of cover up by men and women at the peak of their careers in almost every field. Even with his particular focus on the celebrities who made New York their home, he had not found any evidence of fact, or even rumor, that Matt was in any way a part of the "gay underground" as he had referred to the group of people who had been the topic of the article.

At this point Reese became glaringly aware that the three drinks he had already consumed were no longer numbing the slight nip in the air. The fact that he left his jacket at the table sealed the deal. He pressed his way back into the restaurant and made his way, past some second tier New York icons, to the table where he found his friends sitting amongst numerous empty glasses and a devoured plate of the eatery's famous fries.

"So, who are you fucking?" Benjie slurred in a louder and deeper voice than usual.

"It was my editor, jackass. You know how he always calls. You'd think that I frequently missed deadlines or something."

"Sure it was," Taylor offered in her most patronizing tone. "Whenever you wanna tell me who you're getting freaky with, you just come whisper in Taylor's pretty little ear."

"Jesus, Benjie, what have you done to her? I've seen Tay this drunk before. Hell, it's how we made it through second year, but did you have to give her a shot of your lack of tact as well?"

"You don't have to hide it from us babe. I've been hoping to see you hop back up on the horse for months now. You let that prick affect too much of your life already," Benjie responded.

"Nice choice of words Benjie, and I've told you about a thousand times before that Adam is not the reason I haven't been playing the field. I just haven't felt like it. I need some Reese time before I can go investing myself in someone else."

"Hon, all guys aren't like him. If anyone at this table has a right to be bitter, it's me. I'm a straight girl in Manhattan, the opportunities for me to even have sex—no less, a relationship—with a good-looking guy are worse odds than winning the lottery. You guys have a bigger field to play on. That just means there are gonna be more assholes, but there will be more winners."

"I know they're not all like 'The Bastard,' a.k.a. Adam, I've just got to take it slow to get back into this game."

"See, I knew it, you are seeing someone!" Benjie bellowed.

The rest of the meal was occupied mostly by joking accusations from Benjie, sappy pick-me-ups from Taylor and Reese convincing the two that they were extremely drunk. They all were beginning to sound a bit too much like characters from *Dawson's Creek* and needed to go home.

After stepping out at the corner of 51st and 9th from his taxi, Reese quickly avoided the heckles of the neighborhood gay bar populated by older men who always attempted to court the younger sect as they strolled by.

Quickly downing three glasses of water upon entering his apartment, Reese submitted to the siren call of his lonely bed. With only the clapping of the horse-drawn cabs striking the street, he climbed between his soft cotton sheets and wished they were warm. As he moved toward sleep, he thought of the last person who warmed his bed. Adam had been gone more than four months, but the embarrassment of the loss still stung Reese. How had Reese not known what was going on? He hadn't been blinded by love; they hadn't gotten there yet. He thought he was an observant person, but he definitely missed all the warning signs for that one.

Continuing to analyze the betrayal for about the six millionth time, Reese waited for sleep to come. He believed the best part of falling asleep was the moment right before one loses consciousness. He enjoyed the idea that the next thing he would remember would be waking up. Drifting ever closer to the edge of the unconsciousness cliff, Reese heard his own voice softly chant, "Send in Matt! Send in Matt!"

Chapter Eight

Taylor and Reese exited their cab at Rivington and Essex in Manhattan's Lower East Side under a light early spring rain. The Tuesday night traffic had made them more late than they had hoped to be when they had decided to be fashionable and not eager.

"There it is," Reese called out while trying to shield Taylor from the drops of water assaulting her perfectly aligned hair and pointing to Gallery 27, named in reference to Matt's jersey number for the New York Knicks.

Entering the cavernous industrial space, they were welcomed by who they would later learn was Gallery 27's managing partner, Gilda Wentworth.

Once Gilda recognized Reese and Taylor as "Gibbons +1" on her guest list, she ushered them along the concrete and white wall hallway to one of the gallery's main showrooms. It was the opening of a new artist from the Bronx who sculpted celebrity likenesses with a clear paper mache from wallpaper. Standing on its pedestal before Reese and Taylor as they were handed glasses of wine, was the likeness of Bill Clinton constructed from a mixture of Great American President wallpaper and one made with little blue dresses.

Reese was scanning the room, looking for Gilda's partner, and hopefully his own, while trying to drown out Taylor's ramblings.

"What do you think this is trying to say?" Taylor asked in her most pseudo-intellectual voice. "Is the artist saying that Bill would be considered one of the greatest presidents if it wasn't for

Monica? Or is he saying that he is one of the greatest despite the headline-grabbing whore?"

"I don't know," he said as he downed his glass of Cabernet Sauvignon like he was knocking back a shot of tequila at a tea dance on Fire Island.

"Honey, slow down," Taylor exclaimed. "We're among the artsy hoity-toity. Don't be falling into a cab too quickly this evening, 'cause I wanna meet your hot new *straight* friend."

Just as her words broke into the space around the two, Reese's eyes met Matt. He was standing with a model he had seen before. Reese assumed this was Alex clinging to his right arm while talking to Heath and a few faux art critics who were hanging on the gallery owner's every word.

It was the first time Reese had laid eyes on Matt since that day in the hotel room in Philadelphia. "Damn he looks good," Reese thought to himself as he studied the finely tailored dark suit that decorated his finely tuned physique. As much as Reese wanted to run up to him and say hello, he knew that was as good of an idea as going over and smacking him a kiss while grabbing his crotch.

Reese decided to play it cool and wait for his host to make the first move and grabbed another glass of wine, turning his attention back towards Taylor. "Oh there he is, Tay. See him against . . . What is that a sculpture of? Charlie's Angels?"

"I think that's supposed to be The Hansons. Let's go check it out," she offered, "and you can introduce me to your new friend."

"Why don't we wait?" he asked, trying to hide the terror of the moment. "It looks like he's busy, and he'll make the rounds. He did call and ask us to come. Plus, he's with his roommate, Heath, and I believe the woman is Matt's date Alex."

"What's the big deal? As you said, he invited you," she said as Matt looked up, catching Reese's gaze. The smile was instantaneous on both of their faces. Matt's arm shot up to wave but was quickly pulled back down as his face abruptly turned stiff, remembering where he was.

It was a minimal break of character, Reese thought. No one noticed.

"Here he comes, Tay," Reese said. "Now be nice."

"Oh, I'll be nice, fret not."

Closing in on his guests, Matt's walk became more stern and rigid. He offered his hand to Reese and with a slight smile as his façade, he said, "Reese. Welcome. I'm so glad you could come." Taken aback by this frosty welcome, Reese could only mutter, "This is my friend Taylor. She beat my dog while we were in Philadelphia."

"I did not beat Logan!" Taylor yelled in her defense. "The magazine rack just happened to fall on him while I was scolding him for eating my shoes."

"It was a bookcase," Reese corrected.

"You know it's not nice to hit a defenseless dog," Matt said, trying to lighten the mood, yet hide his excitement in seeing Reese. The two men had spoken briefly while he was on the road and he thought everything was fine. Maybe he shouldn't have tried to see him in public so soon. Hopefully, Reese would understand the role both of them had to play.

Looking coldly at Reese, Taylor quipped, "Well, if he wasn't thrust into my car as a last resort, maybe I would still have a few cute shoes in my closet."

"OK, Tay. We get the picture," Reese attempted to reason as he turned his attention to his secret lover. "How is the opening going?"

"I think it's going well," Matt conceded before elaborating that Gilda was at her wit's end in dealing with the temperamental artist who failed to show. "I think two pieces already sold."

"Someone bought this crap?" Taylor said not realizing that her inner monologue hadn't been turned off. "I'm sorry, Matt. I didn't mean it that way."

"Oh, I agree," he said as he continued to explain that in the New York art world, a statement must be made by the galleries so they can have the buzz necessary to get the hot artists to commit to their space. "I think this is a bunch of crap, but I also think it's kind of funny."

"It is," she confirmed. "It looks like Madame Tussaud's Wax Museum on crack."

"But there is something about seeing both of the George Bushes being plastered with Homer Simpson wallpaper," Reese countered.

"You're not going to give this more publicity are you?" Taylor argued before noticing Matt's eager smile to the thought of his gallery gaining more attention.

"Why not?" Reese said in disbelief to Taylor not believing that it would be a great topic for his column. "It's the complete idiocracy that my readership loves and I can relate to. No offense, Matt."

"None taken," he said as he excused himself from the group with a bright smile in the quibbling friends' direction.

As they found a deserted corner in the rear of the gallery, Taylor whispered, "He's *so* on your team."

"What?"

"I bet he was one of those guys in high school who ordered the Soloflex video when he was younger so he could watch that hunk of a man sweat," she continued. "I bet you, he jacked off to it, too. Being an athlete was the perfect cover. But all you boys have that video. Hell, I'm sure I could still find it in the movie collection in your den."

"Of course, I have that video," Reese conceded. "I consider it my first porn. But, I'm sorry to tell you, babe, he's on your team. We can't have all the good-looking ones. What makes you think that he's not straight?"

"He was cold to me during our introductions," Taylor explained. "He was eager to see you from across the room, but was very reserved when he approached us. It was like too much of a cover."

"He thought you were a dog beater," Reese argued.

"And then, look at Anna, that girl who was draped all over him earlier."

"Alex," Reese corrected. "She models for J. Crew."

"Whatever," she continued. "Look at her. She's now all over the other guy."

"Heath," he offered. "I met him in Philadelphia, too. Nice guy."

"Well, she's totally flirting all five feet eleven inches of herself all over him now. That beard definitely needs to learn what it means to be a cover."

After gathering a few stuffed shrimp from the attentive wait staff, Reese turned to find Alex and Heath nearly upon himself and Taylor. "You should like Heath. Wall Street type, but somewhat enlightened."

Reese didn't actually witness any of the "enlightenment" that he just claimed Heath possessed. He was just sure that if he helped shield his best friend's sexuality, Heath couldn't be like the thousands of traders and investment bankers that the new hetero urban male had become. Hunting having been replaced by their health club memberships and their stock options in the stead of land grants from the king, the new breeder boy of Manhattan had steadfastly maintained his male chauvinistic and homophobic attitudes.

"Hello, I'm Alexandra, a friend of Matt, and this is Heath," she offered as the new foursome started with fresh glasses of wine all around. "I believe you know him, Reese."

"We go way back," Heath snorted.

"Yes, long lost friends reunited," Reese said merrily.

"Do you two need anything?" Alex said while pulling a peeled shrimp from the passing waitress.

"We're fine," Taylor said coldly. "We were just discussing the exhibit. We wondered how much crack must have been smoked to come up with such a preposterous exhibit."

"Forgive Taylor," Reese offered, "being a daughter of a conservative Republican Senator, she believes she's entitled to voice her somewhat tainted views, no matter how out of place they may be."

"I'm quite liberal," she explained to Alex and Heath as they sat back and watched the banter play out before them. "But being liberal doesn't mean I don't have taste."

Heath recoiled in laughter as he offered his hand to Taylor, "I don't believe we've met. I'm Heath Fletcher, Matt's friend and roommate."

"Roommate?" Taylor inquired in her usual loud and unapologetic fashion. "Why would a single, good-looking man who plays for the New York Knicks need a roommate?"

"I thought the same thing," Heath said, attempting to defuse Taylor's inquiring mind. "But we've been roommates since college and when he bought a huge loft in SoHo, he wanted someone else to live with him so it wouldn't sit empty while he was on the road."

"That makes sense," Taylor said in resignation.

"Of course it does," Heath said as he gently took her by the arm and led her across the room. "Have you seen the sculpture of Steven Spielberg made out of candy cane wallpaper?"

Heath had removed Taylor so easily from the group Reese was left standing next to Alex, wondering what had happened.

"Heath's good," Alex said in respect to his diplomatic skills before turning and abruptly asking for Reese's address.

"It's for Matt," she said with her best modeling scowl. "He would like to come over tonight after this finishes up. I can give him the address a bit more discreetly than you can."

"Of course," he said as he dug through his sport jacket's pocket for a card. "I had these made up just for times like this."

"For when strange women come up to you as a go-between for your latest trick?" Alex said with a half laugh. "Is there a bar close by where he can tell the driver to drop him off? He can't just say your building or it will end up in the gossip pages. Fuckin' cab drivers."

Reese tried to think of a place, but only could think of the gay bar in the building adjacent to his own. Obviously that wouldn't work. "Oh, tell him Single Room Occupancy," he exclaimed as he could remember one relatively cool, non-gay bar in his increasingly homosexual neighborhood. "It's on 53rd Street between Eighth and Ninth Avenues."

"I know it," she said contemptuously. "That place is so over."

*   *   *

Reese couldn't help but smile when he saw Matt still asleep in his own bed. He had snuck out from his lover's grasp only thirty minutes earlier so he could scurry to the neighborhood Amish Market for fresh milk, butter, eggs and everything else he would need for his new lover's first breakfast by his hands. Now as the clock neared ten, he knew if he was going to have any real time with his new man, he would have to wake him before Matt had to go to practice.

Kneeling at the edge of the bed had made no noticeable difference in Matt as his breath showed no hesitation in his slumber. Reese decided to wiggle up under the kicked open sheets and comforter and give his lover a proper welcome, but as his head moved slowly up Matt's leg he noticed the possum had been playing dead.

Matt quickly clasped Reese between his legs and wrestled him to the foot of the bed ultimately pinning the host on his back. "Did ya think you could sneak up on me? Hmmm," he cried as he began to tickle Reese into submission. "Where did you go? Hmmm." Reese couldn't contain his laughter or his breath as Matt dug his long fingers under his arms.

Finally, when Matt had been declared the Lord of the Bed, Reese admitted his plot to fetching the supplies necessary for a meal worthy for such a Lord and retreated to the kitchen, leaving Matt to scan the *Times*, *Post* and *Daily News* for information on that night's game.

"Do you remember Chris McIntyre?" Matt asked while lounging in bed with Logan after discovering that the Knicks beat reporters actually knew very little about the coming contest with the Celtics.

"Oh my God! Where did that come from?" Reese screamed, obviously shocked, as he bolted in from the kitchen where he had been carefully separating eggs for what he considered was his world-famous blue cheese and spinach omelet.

"I was just thinking that we went to high school together and there was a good chance both of us started to play with other boys around the same time. Just curious if you 'experimented'

with anyone I knew, or I played with, too." Matt coyly offered as
he flipped through 'The Arts' section of the *Times*, all the while
sipping on the café au lait Reese had bought from the
neighborhood coffee pot.

"So he was your first? Chris McIntyre? You're kidding me."

"Not at all," Matt said, beaming with pride. "Chris and I got
together during Friday Night Live during Senior Follies week.
We were working late on rehearsals and you know."

"No, I don't know," Reese said with a wicked grin. "Go ahead
tell me."

"Oh God," Matt said while putting down the paper and arching
his neck back to rest his head upon the black wrought-iron
headboard. "Chris and I were doing Hans and Frans and we
were working late on the costumes. He was working on the
padding forever and was adamant that we stitch them into our
clothing. In retrospect, I think he was just trying to spend more
time together."

Reese could hardly contain his excitement as he crawled
back on to his bed and sat Indian style with baited breath. "So
then what happened?"

"Well, we were kinda feeling each other up through all the
padding until we actually started to grope each other."

"Well, with all that rubbing, you had to have gotten hard at
some point." Reese rationalized.

"Exactly, well, soon enough we were going down on each
other that night in the prop room. I remember he came after like
two thrusts of entering my mouth.

"The prop room. That's great," Reese said as he returned to
his kitchen and his stiffening egg mixture.

"Yeah, so what about you?" Matt asked eagerly following his
host into the kitchen.

"What do you mean?" Reese said as he poured his creation
into a sizzling hot pan, releasing a powerful plum of smoke that
masked the manly scent of wicked sex that pervaded the entirety
of the apartment.

"Come on, I told you," Matt whined.

"All right, all right," Reese succumbed. "Well, do you remember Chris McIntyre?"

"No way! When?"

"Yearbook final deadline, Art Room number two, April 14, 4:15 P.M."

"At least it didn't make an impression on you," Matt said sarcastically.

"He was a photographer for us at the paper and had been doing extra shots for a soccer story, since he was on the team. We were going over some of his negatives, and it just kind of happened."

"So what happened then?"

"You cheeky bastard! You want details. Well, I would like to say that I held out to my third or fourth date, but I can't. You know me too well for that lie," Reese said sticking his tongue out with glee. "Let's just say that my feet were in the air with my back on a table as he plowed away. I think we used some cream moisturizer as lube. I couldn't sit for a week."

As Matt tried to pick his jaw up from the floor, Reese continued, "Chris McIntyre paved my road to freedom, so to speak. I think he picked up on my sexual persuasion a lot earlier than others."

"We can spot our own," Matt said as Reese presented him with a plate adorned with a perfect omelet, some fresh fruit and a glass of no-pulp orange juice fortified with calcium. "This looks delicious, you didn't tell me you were a cook as well."

"Why thank you. I once considered culinary school—I've always enjoyed cooking—but I realized I could never see myself as a full-time chef," he said as they settled into the bay window kitchen nook overlooking the courtyard shared by the building. "Well, I agree with you that we can spot our own now. Back then was another thing entirely."

"I wonder where he is now?" Matt asked as he finished his coffee and dug into his breakfast.

"He's a bartender at JR's in Washington. Unfortunately, he hasn't stopped having sex with 18-year-old guys. Supposedly, he's a major chicken hawk. But we should give the guy some credit for spotting the two of us in that bastion of breederism. Was that one time in the prop room your only time with him?"

"No, we developed a regular thing for a few months," Matt explained. "It wasn't even anything more than sex, considering he was dating Jessie Linden at the time. He would just suck me off once or twice a week. Why? Did you guys become a thing?"

"Like you, nothing emotional—just sex. Every Wednesday night he would come over and we would go at it in my basement. Of course I finally bought lube, because I was making too much noise from using Lubriderm or any other lotion I could find."

"Didn't your parents figure it out?"

"I don't think so," Reese said. "While my parents are totally cool with my life now, at the time they had their heads buried in the sand. I think they probably heard things, but made rationalizations of the sounds like 'Oh, it's the dog.'"

"The dog?"

"I'm fucking serious, I just told them I also heard the noise and figured it was one of our dogs chasing something around the fence outside. They always were eager to accept that."

Reese had always wondered if his parents actually believed that the dog was capable of making moans of passion. He knew that his parents were quite capable of letting themselves believe whatever they needed to be happy, but ignoring distinct noises from the basement was a little extreme. Perhaps they knew the whole time, and were just waiting for him to be comfortable with telling them. Maybe they just wanted to be fair.

"Denial can be such a happy place," Matt said while rolling his eyes and polishing off his omelet.

"Well if anyone can understand the joys of denial it has to be you. Right up until the moment when my dick was in your mouth I had no idea you were gay."

"I think you need to get your gaydar fixed, 'cause I thought I was being pretty obvious ever since we sat down for dinner."

"I have a feeling my gaydar was encountering some interference from my wishdar."

"Oh really?" Matt smirked.

"Yeah, but that's not a problem anymore. Wish granted. Signal clear. You're a big 'ole fag," Reese said, giggling.

"Very funny. Compared to you I'm a butch professional athlete. Oh wait, I am!"

"But you didn't know you were gay at the Academy, right?" Reese asked. "So, how did you deal with your weekly sessions with Chris?"

"I just convinced myself that what we were doing was normal, and that so long as I didn't do it with other guys, or kiss him, it was just playing around," he reasoned. "It wasn't until later when I started to realize why I wasn't having that good of a time sleeping with girls and wanted to be with boys a lot more."

"So when did that happen?" Reese asked in his most inquisitive tone.

"Well my first two years of college I was still fighting things, like not staring at Matthew McConaughey's ass too much while he was walking up the steps in that Grisham movie *A Time to Kill*."

"That's not possible!" Reese shrieked. "I drool every time I even think about that scene. Neither he nor an ass has ever looked that good in khaki again."

"Tell me about it. Between that scene, the release of the Abercrombie & Fitch catalogs, and my growing sexual frustration resulting from my continued bad sex with women, I don't know how I managed so long."

"How no one really knows about anyone in high school, or even in college, is just a testament to the fact that we're not as important in everyone else's lives as we think we are," Reese reasoned. "I always thought people were watching everything I did, listening to every word I said, noticing who I was looking at. In my mind, the entire world cared what I did."

"I think that's called paranoia."

"Oh, it's total paranoia, but for a good reason. I mean, to me it was one helluva secret. So does anyone know your secret, besides Heath, Alex and myself?"

"As you guessed, Alex is my quote-unquote beard and Heath has been helping me out since third year at school when I forgot to clear my Internet history."

Reese rolled with laughter as Matt continued his story of when Heath typed the "g" for GoStanford.com, and Gay.com popped up in the navigation bar of his Explorer window. "When I got home that afternoon, he just asked me flat out. He's very direct like that, which is good for me 'cause I always know where I stand."

"Did he look pissed?"

"No, he was all right. But once I started to date he helped cover for me."

"So are they, and now myself, the only ones who know about your dirty little secret?" he asked with an evil grin while sitting upon Matt's lap.

"Wayne, you met him in Philly, he knows. He's my best friend on the team, so we've got each other's backs. My agent suspects. That's about it, except for some random people."

"Random people like the people you've dated?" Reese asked, trying to make it sound like part of the conversation, while it was mostly just personal research.

"Well yeah, but there haven't been that many of those," Matt said as he began to laugh at the thought of his few and far in-between romances. "Most people can't handle the schedule, or the sneaking around. And it's hard to meet people when you can't exactly walk into a gay bar. The sports industry isn't overflowing with men on our team, so it becomes a matter of trust."

"So why do you trust me?"

"Because it doesn't seem like work."

Chapter Nine

"I don't know why you're so damn eager to take me," Taylor said in disgust as their cab sped down Ninth Avenue. "I mean, I did the fucking gallery thing. Why couldn't you get Benjie or your editor to go with you?"

"Oh yeah, I'm going to take Benjie to a Knicks game," Reese said with a laugh. "Can you imagine? He would cry having to sit next to whatever stereotypical Westchester resident would be destined to be there. Benjie would go to the mattresses for the arm rest, for sure."

Reese also had an ulterior motive for bringing Taylor along to Matt's game. After meeting her at Gallery 27, Heath was interested in seeing her again. Of course, Taylor would have had nothing to do with Heath, if Reese had asked. She believed Heath to be a pretentious snob with nothing of merit to deserve another look.

But Matt convinced Reese that Heath wasn't too much of a womanizer. And in Reese's mind, Taylor needed some action anyway, if she were ever to get so lucky. So, he decided to throw his friend to the wolves, or wolf in this case.

Exiting the cab and making their way to the player's entrance off 33rd Street, Reese and Taylor were greeted by three security guards and two employees of Madison Square Garden who handled tickets for the player's friends and family, as well as servicing the arriving media members. Noting *Post* writer Kevin Ashbie being worked over by one of the guards, Reese quickly passed by and into the waiting elevator.

"A friend of yours?" Taylor asked as she witnessed Kevin being thoroughly humiliated by having his bag, jacket, pants and shoes taken off and searched in a very thorough manner. "I wish airport security was that anal."

"He writes for the *Post*," Reese said without trying to mention more about Kevin and the sensitivity that was required to avoid him as much as possible.

The two found their seats as the shoot-around session of warm-up ended. They were situated eight rows back from the Knicks' bench and in perfect position to see Matt take a few extra eighteen-foot jump shots before heading to courtside. Seconds after hearing his last-minute instructions from a slew of assistant coaches, Matt looked up and found his two player-owned seats filled by Reese and Taylor.

"Oh look, he sees us!" Taylor squealed before standing and shouting "Hi Matt!"

As she continued to wave her arms around as if she was suffering some spontaneous epileptic seizure, Reese offered, "He's at work, Taylor. Do you want him to come to your office on Fifth Avenue and wave to you during a Clinique staff meeting?"

"With guns like that he can do whatever he wants," she said with lust in her voice.

"So, now your story's changed, eh?"

Before Taylor had the chance to respond, the main lights went off within the Garden and spotlights started "searching" through the interior of the arena as loud music played at a deafening level. To a rain of boos and jeers from the stands, the Celtics were introduced one after another.

When the crowd began to clap in unison to a more upbeat song synchronized with a video playing on the JumboTron above the court, Reese felt as if he was a part of something special. One by one the hometown Knicks were introduced by the most baritone voice the announcer could muster. On the announcer's fourth call, Reese couldn't breathe as he heard, "And now, a six-foot-five-inch guard from Stanford University, number twenty-seven, Matt Walker."

The words rung in Reese's ears as he felt the drama and the power within them. A six-foot-five-inch guard from Stanford, Reese thought to his merriment. How did he get so lucky? Even when saying his name, the announcer stressed its magnitude by dragging the syllable of "Matt" before a stiletto-styled "Walker" with the "r" being held and fading before the final Knick was introduced.

Matt Walker, Reese thought to himself, the man that he loved and adored, was treated so special within these walls. But, how could Reese ever compete?

As he contemplated his own question, Heath stumbled across Taylor to sit in between the two friends. "Sorry, I'm late," he said before signaling to the beer man for a round of three.

"I didn't know you were coming," Taylor said, shooting a look of death towards Reese. "Did you know Heath was going to be here tonight, Reese?"

Ignoring his friend, Reese took a beer from Heath and made himself comfortable for the game. "So break it down for us, Heath."

Heath explained that tonight was a critical game for the Knicks, if not a critical matchup for Matt. The Celtics were well positioned for the approaching playoffs while the Knicks were three games out of being the last team selected from the Eastern Conference.

"Matt's got a tough forty-eight minutes in front of him," he said. "He'll be going up against Paul Pierce from Kansas. Pierce has been on fire since the All-Star game and is averaging nearly thirty points a night. I think Matt can score on him, but I don't know if he can stop Pierce defensively."

Not long after the ball was tipped, the trio, as well as the rest of the world saw exactly what Heath had meant by saying that Pierce was on fire. Taking the ball on the Celtics' first possession, he drained a three-point shot from off the left side when Matt couldn't fight through a screen, and less than a minute later he stripped Matt of the ball and strolled to the opposite basket and slammed it home. Before anyone had exhaled from the pre-game introductions, the Celtics were up ten to two.

Matt looked very uncomfortable on the floor moving indecisively as he scored no points on three shots in the first quarter and the crowd began to notice. Thankfully, most of the Knicks turned in horrible showings as they fell to a twenty-six-point halftime deficit.

"Damn," Heath uttered as he tried to make some sense of the night's game in his head. "This is his first start at home. He could be nervous. But I haven't seen him off this much in my entire life."

In the second half Matt's performance didn't improve as he continued to struggle from the field. When he finally made a steal off the Celtic guard and looked to make his first bucket of the night on a fast break lay up, an opposing forward came from behind and swiped the ball cleanly away from him.

A rain of boos began to fall on the court as the Garden erupted against their new starting guard. Heckles directed at Matt could be heard from far and near, but it wasn't until a young banker type dressed in a white oxford shirt and blue jeans sitting two rows behind Taylor made his voice heard that Reese really began to worry.

"Fuckin' faggot!" the man stood and shouted. "Get off the court and go down the street to Chelsea with the rest of the queers."

Taylor seemed to be unfazed by the outburst, but Reese's eyes bugged and stirred uncomfortably within his skull. Heath, however, couldn't sit still and listen to some asshole fuck with his friend in this very public way. He had heard it too many times from too many drunken bastards who had never played the game they watched religiously. Heath didn't want to hear it anymore.

"What the fuck is your problem? He's having a bad night," Heath shouted back with a cold look upon his face.

His plea fell on deaf ears as the man ignored him and continued his rant before sitting back in his seat surrounded by his horde of followers.

During the next trip down the floor, Wayne broke the Celtic pressure defense and set Matt up for an uncontested mid-range jumper on the right side. The ball rimmed out.

The man was now enraged. "Goddamn son of a bitch!! Stop taking it up the ass and get your head in the game! Jesus Christ!"

His friends hooted in agreement, but Heath's leg began to pump up and down as the man continued, "Only a coach like ours would put a fag on the floor when there is an All Star on the bench! Walker is probably suckin' his dick! Or takin' it up the ass!"

The man thrusted the air with his hips in the direction of the row of seats between himself and Heath before gathering a few high fives from the men around him. Heath became infuriated. He stood from his seat in between Taylor and Reese and leapt across the row of seats that divided the men.

Grabbing the man's throat firmly with his hands, Heath screamed, "What the fuck is your problem?" Apparently Heath didn't notice the irony.

The previous onlookers and neighbors of the two men began to pull them apart. Reese collected a heavy kick to the face when he attempted to reign in Heath's violently waling lower limbs. Finally, when security arrived, Heath was dragged away with his curly hair disheveled and his dress shirt torn open, revealing his firm chest and upper abdominals. Reese wasn't into getting beaten up or looking to give out "rough love," but he had to admit to himself that Heath's actions and appearance thereafter was one of the sexiest things he'd seen, apart from Matt Walker.

"Should we go with him?" Taylor asked Reese as the two noticed play had stopped on the court to watch the sideshow being played out in rows 8 through 10 behind the home bench.

"I guess we should," he said while making eye contact for the first time in the night with Matt who now stood no further than twenty feet from him. Reese offered a shrug of his shoulders before gathering Heath's coat and ushering Taylor into the aisle away from the court.

*   *   *

After getting the go-ahead from Heath as he was being

processed for assault and disorderly conduct, Taylor and Reese departed for Babbo, a trendy restaurant in Greenwich Village, for a late supper. Heath said he would be along once he "removed the NYPD plunger from his ass," and would join Matt in a cab once he cleared his media commitments. Matt and Reese had planned on the four of them having dinner together to allow Taylor to interact with Matt, and more importantly, Heath to interact with Taylor.

Of course that was the plan before Heath became a vigilante.

While it had been Reese's intention to tell Taylor about his relationship with Matt that evening, he was caught off guard by the night's events and his news was more relevant than he had originally anticipated. He reprimanded himself for having to "out" Matt to Taylor in a somewhat direct and trashy manner while scurrying down Seventh Avenue in Omar Akbahd's cab.

He reasoned that it would come out sooner rather than later, considering the current set of circumstances, if he didn't tell her. Reese knew that Taylor wouldn't appreciate being left in the dark, so he had to break Matt's trust and tell her.

But before he could utter the statement, she asked, "Don't you think that Heath was unavoidably delicious?"

Continuing to look out on the deserted sidewalks along Seventh Avenue in a dreamy fashion, she said, "He took action for his friend, and that says a lot for him. I mean I know you couldn't do anything—or wouldn't have. It's not in your nature, Reese, especially since you're fucking Matt. But it is in Heath's. He's a good friend, don't you think?"

Feeling like he had just taken a punch to the stomach, Reese wallowed in his own thought before asking, "How did you know?"

"Oh Honey!" Taylor squealed. "You can't keep anything from me. I've been playing with you since your call from the train. Remember, I'm the cat and you're my ball of string."

Reese laughed while wondering how he ever thought he could keep his relationship with Matt on the down low and off Taylor's radar. She knew him better than anyone in the world, and although he hated her veiled comments to her 'superiority' over him, he knew he could always do the same right back to her. "So you sleeping at Heath's place with Matt and myself or are you going to make him trek uptown to your estate on the Upper East Side?"

As they made their way inside to the extravagant wine bar for a few glasses they heard a man discussing the "brawl" at Madison Square Garden. According to the man, whom Reese and Taylor eavesdropped on, the assailant had been Matt Walker's secret lover. Matt had denied comment on the matter, but the man who was attacked said that he planned to not only press charges against his attacker, but sue the attacker and Matt Walker, as well.

Reese and Taylor sat in silence not knowing what the rest of the night held for them. And while they made small talk about Benjie and his latest antics, the two secretly found it incredibly sexy that they were in the middle of such a brouhaha.

When Matt and Heath walked into the restaurant nearly an hour later, there wasn't a smile to be found. Again, Matt offered his hand to Reese. But while the shake at Gallery 27 had lingered, this one had not. A brisk up and down motion was all that Matt would allow before placing his right hand back into his rain jacket.

The quartet was told their table was ready in an out-of-the-way cubbyhole where distractions would be limited. Reese quickly moved into the seat adjacent to Matt's left side nearly shoving Taylor against the wall.

But again, Reese noticed how tonight's events in rows eight to ten behind the home bench in the Garden had put a damper on everyone's spirits when he tried to rub his leg against Matt's and he pulled it promptly away.

"Kevin was seated right behind you," Matt said, releasing a tightly held breath. "In the post game, he asked about the three of you and not me going two-for-fourteen for the night. I'm sure it's going to be in the goddamn *Post* tomorrow morning."

"Did the Knicks or the Garden release any information on the issue?" Taylor asked.

"They asked me for a statement," Heath offered. "I said 'no comment.'"

"So hopefully, it will go away," Reese said, knowing that they wouldn't be so lucky.

Knocking back the last of his scotch and soda, Heath continued, "The same fuckin' publicist, who asked me to make a statement, went up to the asshole who I went after. I don't know what he said, but they did talk longer than it takes to say 'no comment.'"

Matt held his head low and said, "I just wish this would go away."

"Honey, it's not that big of a deal," Reese said before realizing he had overstepped his bounds.

"You have no fucking idea what just happened do you?" he asked rhetorically. The question frightened Reese and he was taken aback by Matt's change in tone from being one of the defenselessly indicted to responsively aware. Reese felt he should raise his warning level to DEFCON three. "Kevin is going to have this in his story tomorrow."

"I don't see what the big deal is," Taylor interjected. "It's not like fights don't break out in the stands every day."

Turning to face her Matt continued, "He will find out what happened. He will know what was said. He will write about it. He will start the witch hunt."

Heath covered Taylor's hand with his own and explained, "This will be an undeniable event where the press can link the rumors of Matt being gay and not be liable for it. They've never been able to say anything directly connecting the two before this. Now I've given them the ammunition they need to 'out' a New York Knick."

*   *   *

That night when Matt and Reese made their way to bed, it was obvious to both of them that neither wanted to have sex. But the two men didn't want to disappoint each other and accelerate the tension that had developed, so they submitted to their physical desires.

The foreplay had gotten off course. Reese tried every trick while trying to stimulate Matt into an erection. Finally after spending nearly twenty minutes breathing through his nose, Matt began to moan with pleasure, as Reese could no longer take him completely in his mouth. Within moments Matt had entered his lover from behind and began thrusting frantically and without mercy as Reese attempted to relax and enjoy the sensation. But it was to no avail and Reese laid there being pounded into submission.

When Matt had come, he rolled off Reese, sighed and with a vacant look at the ceiling fell asleep.

Chapter Ten

Matt awoke with Reese dancing to Celine Dion's latest hit on VH1's CardioVideo. At the foot of Matt's king-sized bed, Reese's ass shook a bit quicker than the beat of the music. But to Matt's satisfaction, the beauty and firmness of Reese's backside more than made up for his white man's overbite attempt at dancing.

"I never liked Celine Dion," Matt snorted while wiping the sleep from his eyes. "She's all about that wide-leg power shot with the camera looking up to her. It's such a 'cooter shot.'"

"Cooter shot?" Reese said, breaking from his dancing routine. "Is that a reference to her *thing*?"

"Yeah," Matt continued. "It's like, do I need to see that?? If I were into having pussy in my face, I would go to the strip bars with Wayne and the rest of the guys. God knows, I don't need to have Celine's power pussy camera shot while she double pumps her fist against her chest this early in the morning."

"Eww, you didn't just say the p-word!!" Reese exclaimed. "That is such a bad, bad word."

"And 'penis' isn't?" Matt inquired.

"Not at all . . . They're fun!" Reese said honestly. "But, did I ever tell you my theory on that region on the womenfolk?"

As Matt rolled his eyes back, waiting to hear yet another round of Reese's opinions on the minutia of life, he heard his lover ask, "Well, do you remember the Sand Pit with the tentacles in *The Return of the Jedi*?"

"God, no!" Matt shouted as he burst into laughter. "Didn't it make a sound, too?"

"Yeah, it growled. The sad fact is that when I was having sex with a girl for the only time in my life, in college, you know, I had to experiment. Well, that's all I could think about. The sand monster. The growl. The tentacles. The fact that it ate the Storm Trooper. So I started to freak 'cause my dick was down in there. Inside that!" he said, stopping to get a drink of water. "I just came as quickly as I could and got the hell out."

"Oh my God, how could you concentrate with that visual?" Matt said, mocking Reese's enthusiasm.

"Well, it wasn't really a problem," Reese explained while maneuvering his body against Matt's. "Remember it was college and I was nineteen years old. I think the friction of my boxers, at that time, could make me come."

Reese stroked Matt's chest suggestively in order to show him it might take a little more than his boxers, or currently his new uberstylish 2(x)ist boxerbriefs, to get him off this time. But Matt was quick to move off the bed before claiming the need to get up and "face the music."

He motioned toward his laptop lying alongside a lonely chair in his expansive bedroom when a cell phone started to make its presence known.

"Damnit, it's Ira," Matt said after finding his phone tucked in the hip pocket of the jeans he had worn the night before.

Ira Pilton was Matt's agent and was considered one of the best within the League. Ira recruited Matt as a client not for his future as a basketball professional, in fact Ira believed, like most, that Matt was destined to a ho-hum career before being sent out to pasture. But Ira needed Matt for his own mental health. He didn't need another superstar client who would demand 24-hour attention or another one needing to be bailed out of jail every other week. No, Ira wanted Matt so he could say not all athletes were bad.

As Reese sat back in Matt's bed, he wondered if it was all right for him to shower or even be in the room. From the tone of Matt's side of the conversation, Ira was up to speed on the events from the night before.

Reese didn't want to get up and fix breakfast because that might appear insensitive to the issues Matt was discussing on the phone. But was he supposed to just sit there, leaning against the headboard of Matt's bed, and listen to one side of the conversation? He thought Matt would most certainly tell him everything that occurred on the call if he left. Reese could always say that he wanted to give Matt some privacy, but didn't this affect him too? Finally, Reese decided to stay put and pulled a pillow up to shield him from the anticipated fallout.

"Well, it's only mentioned in the 'Notes' section of Kevin's story, but it has been picked up by the Associated Press, so it's on all the websites now," Matt said while tossing his ridiculously small cell phone onto the dresser. "Ira says there is no recourse. It doesn't constitute libel or slander by the paper, because the man Heath attacked gave them a blow-by-blow account of the whole incident. Since Heath didn't say anything to contradict it, which I guess is to the best, they ran with the other guy's story."

"That should be it, right?" Reese hoped more than asked.

"God no," Matt said as he sat down on the edge of the bed. His head sunk into his hands, which were supported by his elbows on his knees. It seemed as if the weight of the world was literally crushing him. Finally, he said meekly, "It's just beginning."

Reese crawled to Matt and placed his right hand along his back. As he stroked, he asked himself should he be golden and stay silent. He decided he shouldn't. "I'm sure it won't be as bad as you think it will."

Matt turned his head toward his boyfriend, showing his look of contempt. "You have no fucking idea, do you?"

Matt stood and began to pace through his bedroom, explaining how this would open the proverbial Pandora's box. "The media love this issue because the conservatives can use it as a platform to condemn homosexuality and the liberals can use it to condemn the conservatives and athletes in general. This is going to be everywhere! Remember when *Out*'s Brendan Lemon wrote his trite editorial disclosing his relationship with a professional athlete? Everyone wrote about it—including you!"

Finally caught in his hypocrisy, Reese fell silent. He knew it was true. Reese had written the column considered as the gay community's response to Lemon's editorial, laying into the *Out* editor for introducing the volatile topic yet refusing to bring anyone forward to be sacrificed. Reese was also very critical of the "major league baseball player" Lemon claimed he had been romantically involved with. He openly wondered if said player even existed.

Now as Reese sat in the bed of his own closeted professional-athlete boyfriend, Reese had to consider just how big of a hypocrite he had become. Did sleeping with his high school crush affect him that much? He now perpetuated the closeted life he wrote was a blight upon gay society. His entire view on gay closeted celebrities had been shaken apart.

Could he fix it, he wondered, before asking what had been in the back of his mind since Matt first swallowed his cock back in Philadelphia. "So, why not just get it over with and come out?"

"Jesus Christ!" Matt raged. "Don't you think I've thought of all this before? Don't you think that this one issue occupies ninety percent of my life? I lay awake at night thinking about this!"

"Matt, calm down," he pleaded while taking a step toward him. "If it is as imminent as you believe it is, I'm just wondering if you staying in the closet and being outed is better than coming out and putting your spin on it. It was the same issue that Arthur Ashe faced when he said he was HIV positive."

"Ashe was outed!" Matt said. "The fucking reporter called Ashe and told him that there was a story about to run that he had AIDS. That's not a choice, Reese. That's entrapment."

"I see your point, but he was still able to put his own spin on it and I think he was revered for telling his story in such a classy way."

"He was dying and caught the disease through no fault of his own," Matt said with great indignation. "No gay athlete can ever think that he could compare his coming out to Ashe's experience and expect the world to react the same way."

"But you can learn from it and use it to your advantage,"

Reese offered. "Hello, you're a fucking athlete! You guys walk on water in the eyes of most Americans. By you saying that you're gay, you would be putting the issue in terms that they couldn't ignore."

"Reese, they would see me as the worst type of gay man. I would be the one who hid my sexuality from them. In their eyes, I would have betrayed them. I would be a liar. Almost inhuman."

"The simple fact of the matter is that with you being able to put a ball through a hoop, they would give you the benefit of the doubt," Reese argued. "Plus, you would always have a job."

"You are vastly oversimplifying, again," Matt said with a hint of condescension. "Don't think for one second I would still be 'just one of the team' if I came out. The locker room is a tough place, and I would be labeled as a problem maker. General managers, in response to the homophobic guys on the team, won't mind taking a lesser player as long as team chemistry was not disrupted."

"They say winning is everything, but as long as you're one of them," Matt continued. "You can rape your girlfriend. Hell, you can be a rampant drug user or even a dealer, but you can't love a man. Sports is the last refuge for homophobes in America."

"That must change," Reese said simply.

"Are you asking me to do it?" Matt raged. "Why the fuck should I do it? I've worked too hard for too long to get my shot in the League."

"But they're not letting you be yourself," Reese pleaded. "You can't compromise that."

"Oh, I see," Matt said. "I can compromise my dream of being a professional basketball player, but I cannot compromise my sexuality? You're a fucking hypocrite. The only reason you want me to come out is that it helps your cause of putting the gay agenda in everyone's face. You don't give a damn about it ruining my life and my dreams."

"I didn't say that."

"It sure as hell is what you're implying that I should do," Matt countered. "It's not your life you're asking me to throw away.

You're asking me to do that to mine. Let me ask you, how does it feel from the cheap seats?"

Matt stood and walked away from the bed, turned to Reese and said, "I knew getting involved with you would be a mistake."

Reese sat stunned at what just took place. Listening to the shower beginning to run, he traced the argument in his head from where their little talk of Celine Dion's pussy morphed into an argument on whether Matt should be the trailblazer to the gay community as Jackie Robinson had been to African-Americans.

*   *   *

The city streets were wet from the morning rain when Reese left Matt's SoHo loft. Tucking his dirty blond hair under a stolen baseball cap from Matt's closet, Reese hailed a cab for the trip back uptown.

His eyes were puffy and worn out from the fight earlier in the morning, so he could barely read his cell phone's text messages from Benjie. Entering the cab and directing him north, Reese read that Benjie *had* to meet him for lunch.

Apparently, the producers of *Today* wanted to do a piece on gay athletes, and since Benjie had already gotten a report from Taylor before heading off to a staff meeting at the conclusion of that morning's show, he wanted to check some facts with the source. Convinced Benjie would flaunt the fact that it was "two of his closest friends" who were at the Garden standing up for gay rights, he knew all too well that Benjie would spin the event for the betterment of his career.

Reese didn't know what to do. He knew he couldn't avoid Benjie. Benjie was simply someone who wouldn't abide by being brushed off. Many things could be done to him, Reese thought, but ignoring Benjie was most definitely not one of them.

With a lump in his throat, he knew he would be unable to carry on a conversation at that particular moment. He typed in a quick text message saying, "Ariba! @ 1," and hit the send button before he could chicken out. Maybe he could play it off as if there was no story.

But Reese knew that for him and Matt to succeed he couldn't force the issue. He had nearly pushed too hard that morning, but thankfully when Reese joined Matt in his shower he noticed his lover's eyes were as sad and regretful as his own. They didn't mention the argument again when they both departed for the respective destinations, and a silent understanding now existed.

*   *   *

Reese knew that Benjie would disapprove of his restaurant choice for lunch, but he didn't care. He needed the comfort food and margaritas. Plus the cute, young waiters catering at the gayest Mexican restaurant in Manhattan would surely be a distraction for Benjie. Reese needed every advantage in his favor to pull off this misdirection.

Arriving purposely ten minutes late to further antagonize Benjie, Reese entered the restaurant on the corner where he lived in Hell's Kitchen where he was shuttled to the very last table in the joint. Benjie was sitting alone and halfway through his frozen strawberry margarita.

"That waiter is one of those bitchy queens we see in the movies that we all secretly want to be," Benjie quipped. "But, it's easier to be that 'bitchy queen' when you have a script telling you what to say and the other actors are told not to slap the shit out of you. But if he ever sits us back here again, I'm going to ignore *my* script and pop him in the ass."

"Stop being dramatic," Reese said. "We always end up in the back for some reason. But didn't you pop him in the ass last summer and never see him again?"

"Oh, was that him from the Pines at that one party with you know who?" Benjie asked himself with a little laugh.

Benjie was always amused at how he never recognized his tricks after a week, and quite often had repetitive hookups where he didn't notice the recurring roles until he saw his partner's penis. "I might forget a name or a face, but honey, I'll never forget a cock."

When the waiter Benjie had loved, in one way or another, came back with Reese's first and Benjie's second drink, the youngest producer at *Today* said, "So what the fuck happened?"

"Nothing."

"Oh come on, bitch. Taylor gave me more than that."

"What did she say?"

"She just told me that this guy Heath leapt out at a Jeff Cordero and beat him down at the game."

Reese found it odd that he hadn't heard the man's name before this. Jeff Cordero. He didn't look like a Jeff, but then again, the name didn't seem like one for a homophobe. Reese always thought gay bashers and their kind should have easily recognizable names like Russell, Eugene and Billy Bob. It would make everything so much simpler.

"Did she say why?" Reese asked.

"Because Cordero was calling your boy a fag," Benjie smirked to himself. "So what's up with that? Is he or isn't he?"

"He's not," Reese lied and took a long pull from the straw in his margarita.

"You're lying."

"I am not!"

"Fine," Benjie conceded. "You don't have to tell me, 'cause it's all over your face. You're sleeping with him."

"Wha . . . no." Reese cried, trying to play the outrage card. But Benjie wouldn't have any of it as he just smiled and dug into the chips and salsa that were lying on the table.

"Benjie, you can't tell anyone," Reese said finally. "I'm going to kill that bitch for telling you."

"Oh my God!" he exclaimed. "You are fucking him!"

"What?"

"Taylor didn't tell me a damn thing," he said, brimming with pride. "I ran by your place this morning after the show and you weren't there. I met your neighbor Sharon in the hallway and she said you didn't come home last night. I put two and two together and got a queer three-dollar bill."

"Benjie, you can't tell anyone," Reese said sternly. "Promise me."

"Oh come on, Mister I'm-going-to-out-all-the-fags-in-Hollywood."

"Benjie, I don't know anymore."

"You weren't wrong, Reese. You're just getting fucked and when you're getting fucked, you can't have an agenda."

The two men stared at each other, trying to read their next moves, but Reese knew he couldn't let Benjie go outside with the thought of taking this piece of information to better his career. But since there wasn't a secret anymore Reese told him the whole story, starting with sharing the group shower in high school.

"So this guy is your Holy Grail," Benjie said with a heavy heart. "I had a Holy Grail, too. He was a camp counselor at my youth camp in Vermont. He was sixteen and I was fourteen. I followed him around for an entire summer before he noticed me."

"And when he did, did he beat you down?"

"No, he just came and got me every night after lights out and would let me blow him down on the dock. He now works at National Rent-A-Car outside Boston."

Benjie was a Gay-Straight Alliance pioneer in the early 1990s and can't recall a time when he didn't openly identify himself as gay. So when he told Reese of sucking off his camp counselor in Vermont, Reese knew that it had to be true. Benjie's life was full of enough fabulous stories. He didn't need to dream one up to continue a conversation.

"So what are you going to do?" Benjie asked.

"I'm going to make you promise me that there will be no story on *Today* about this," Reese pleaded.

"That's easy 'cause that was a lie."

"What?"

"I was just fucking with you," Benjie laughed. "We're fucking *Today*. Do you actually think we're into breaking sex scandals? We do puff pieces to make the three blind mice—Katie, Matt and Al—look intelligent and interesting."

"I hate you."

Chapter Eleven

"Matt, I need a hard screen on Francis," Wayne shouted during a timeout versus Houston. "The kid is on me like glue."

Fresh out of a television timeout, Matt fed the ball to Twan as he cut across the lane. Twan had been dating one of the latest hip-hop queens that ruled the pop charts and he could be prone to distraction when she was there. Fortunately for the Knicks, she was not there this night, and Twan took the ball directly to the hole for a bucket and one with a whistle coming last as a member of the frustrated Houston frontcourt made too much contact for the officials to look the other way.

Off the next inbound play, Twan stole the ball from a distracted Rocket and bounced a feed to Wayne who lofted it crosscourt to Matt for a dunk. In less than twenty seconds, the Knicks' lead went from three to seven and the squad was on cruise control as they coasted to their fourth consecutive win.

Numerous reporters had attributed the streak to Matt's injection into the starting rotation and his more steady play over the erratic Anthony Michaels. But Matt had refocused his energies on the court while on a lengthy road trip since the debacle at the Garden more than a week ago. Even the catcalls for Anthony were made less and less.

Now back in New York, Matt has asked Reese not to attend the game as it looked like the Knicks were making their last push to gain admission to the postseason. The fact that Matt's role was key to the team's turnaround didn't go unnoticed and if he could assist in getting the squad into the playoffs for the first time in five years, he knew his contract would put him in a much higher tax bracket.

Thank God for Ira, he thought as he made his way to the locker room in the bowels of the antiquated arena. Ira would fix everything. Hell, he already had. He made Heath's attack on Jeff Cordero disappear with a quick sign of a check and had strong armed writers and editors alike to stop harping on such an "irrelevant issue as one as silly as a drunken brawl in the stands."

Matt was positive it was all over as long as he played by his golden rule: do nothing that will cause unwanted attention out in the open. It was only for a short time anyway until it would ultimately be water under the bridge, as his play would garner him a guaranteed multiyear, multimillion dollar deal.

"They can just fuck themselves then," Matt said to himself as he saw his agent waiting at Matt's locker. Ira had been attempting to engage management in talks of a contract extension since the beginning of the season. When Matt was sitting the bench, management didn't want to talk about anything. When Matt became a starter, management wanted to lock him up in a long-term deal, but Ira then wanted to wait for a better offer. Now, all was quiet as the two parties waited to see how the play-off run would end.

"Great game, Matt," Ira said with his slick smile and piercing dark brown eyes shinning through his stylish wire-rimmed glasses. The look made Matt shudder. While Ira was his knight in shining armor, who would undoubtedly slay the proverbial dragon repetitively for his clients, he wasn't one who Matt really liked to be too close to at anytime. He believed the intensity of the creepiness emitting from his agent would flow directly out of Ira in some thick black goo and somehow find its way to Matt if he wasn't careful.

"Another two assists and you would have had a double-double," Ira continued. "I thought you were there when Antoine started finishing, but then Wayne kept feeding him and you stopped."

"Wayne is our point guard, Ira," Matt said without a hint of emotion. "The offense goes through him. Remember I'm the shooting guard, not the point guard. You do know what position I play, right?"

Laughing off the dig, Ira said, "I'm just saying that if you can beef up your stats, it's going to help me when I talk to the front office."

"You're not going to go Jerry Maguire on me now with that 'help me, help you' crap are you? Hey, Handles!" Matt shouted to a drenched Wayne emerging from the shower, "Do you mind if I take a few more assists from you? You know, it's a contract year and all."

"Matty!! Hell yeah, you're taking too many of my dimes already. Casper, aren't you just supposed to be a shooter? What was that dunk in the fourth? Twan's going to be pissed you're taking his showtime."

Twan, hearing his name, got into the action from his locker by shouting, "Matty, you can slam here and there. You know, Handles, it's equal opportunity."

The locker room burst into laughter as Matt said with a mischievous grin, "Sorry Ira, I tried."

As Ira left he told Matt of some new low-level marketing opportunities tied into various basketball camps over the summer and asked for a few more jerseys to be signed. "I'm going to be down at Scores later with a few of the guys, if you want to talk more," Ira offered. "You know, it might not be a bad thing for team chemistry for you to go to these places once in a while. We could slip it to the gossip pages that you were there and got a lap dance or something."

"I think I get along with everyone just fine. I don't think staring at pussy is going to get me any more free looks at the basket. And secondly, I'm going to forget that you just offered that last part."

When the locker room cleared out, Matt took out his cell phone and called Reese. "Hey honey. I'm done if you want to meet up. I can head home or out for a bit if you want, as long as it's dark." The two decided to meet up at his apartment and he quickly got off the phone as Anthony emerged from the adjoining training room.

Frantic as to what Anthony might have overheard, Matt said, "I didn't know anyone was still here."

"Just 'cause I ain't startin' anymore don't mean I ain't around anymore," Anthony replied with a cold look toward Matt.

"I didn't mean that," Matt pleaded. "I just thought I was alone. Look, I'll see you tomorrow at shoot around."

The cab was cold and the night's damp air cut to Matt's bones for the forty-eight blocks to his apartment. The driver was talking frantically about another time he had an NBA player in his cab. According to the middle-aged driver who claimed to be the equivalent of Michael Jordan in his home country of Indonesia, he once drove two former All-Stars "who had many, many rings, my friend" to a bar on the Lower East Side where two "street walkers" joined them for some oral action.

"Can you believe, my friend? Big stars and they fuck woman I could pay twenty dollars to suck my cock," the cabbie went on. "My dick and theirs in the same place! Isn't America great?"

While thought of the NBA stars going after street-walking prostitutes amused Matt for its sheer absurdity, he did wonder why everyone seemed to be so mystified with the celebrity status. Everyone shits, he thought, even Britney Spears. He concluded that everyone had a story and needed a story to make them feel justified in their role in life. It just happened that most of their stories were fiction.

Matt remained cordial and could only muster a few "hmm's" and "oh really's" every couple of blocks. He hated himself for not using a car service like the rest of the team at times like these.

When he tried to replay his side of the conversation to Reese, he wondered what Anthony could have heard. Did Matt mention his boyfriend by name? If he had, would Anthony think Reese was a guy? Reese could have been a women's name. He concluded that what Anthony might have heard and what conclusions he might have drawn would be as completely random as if he had guessed everything right.

Waiting outside in the rain of his Dominick Street loft in SoHo was Reese. Throwing a ten at the driver and thanking him for the ride, Matt called out, "Why are you waiting down here? I gave you a key for a reason."

"I know, but Heath just walked in with Taylor," Reese said while waiting for his hello kiss. "So I decided to wait for you."

"He doesn't care," Matt said while walking past his lover and into his building. "Heath understands the reason why I gave you that key, and these are the situations that I gave you that key for. And, no one should forget that it's my name on the deed."

Returning to the latest task which Reese had claimed as his own in their relationship, he attempted to lighten the mood. "I didn't mind standing in the rain. I love when it storms in the City. It's very romantic, don't you think?"

"The rain isn't what I'm talking about, Reese."

Safely into their elevator Matt continued, "Look, you know the rules. I can't be seen like that. There are rumors out there, and if I give the press any reason to believe that I like fucking man butt, the taunts that are happening now will be like a drop in the bucket compared to the storm that would come."

"I'm sorry," Reese apologized. "I just didn't think."

"The funny thing is I didn't feel this pressure last month when I wasn't starting."

"Or when you weren't dating me," Reese offered.

"Jesus Christ, Reese!" Matt exclaimed as the elevator came to a stop on the top floor. "Don't be melodramatic. I love you. You love me. Please don't be insecure about this. I can't flaunt my relationships around town like the Breeders can."

Entering the loft, the two men found Heath's pants on the floor and Taylor's dress thrown over the sofa. There were also socks, shirts and jackets marking their path from the door to Heath's bedroom.

"It looks like they want to be able to find their way back to the door, if they get lost," Reese said lightheartedly to where there was no response from Matt. "Oh, come on! It's like breadcrumbs. A path like you're in the woods. That's funny!"

Matt rolled his eyes at his boyfriend and chuckled, allowing himself to breathe again. The two opened a bottle of wine as they sat in the living room while Matt told Reese about his run-in with Anthony in the locker room, as well as his seventeen-point, eight-assist performance on the court.

* * *

Meeting Taylor and Benjie for lunch later in the day, Reese scurried out of Matt's apartment before he woke. In the real world, Heath and Taylor had left hours earlier to make their daily treks to their nine to fives. But with it quickly approaching noon, Reese actually had things to do before the drinking would begin.

Taylor started the Monday Morning Club during her second year in college. The return to class from the weekend was too tough on her spirit, so the trio of friends would schlep down to their local watering hole to knock back more than a few drinks at two o'clock. She reasoned that the hell of Monday's was much easier to take when there was a drink in her hand. Now, the party just shifted to a late, but still rather lengthy alcohol-soaked lunch.

The group's latest destination for their two-hour break from life was Sushi Samba in the West Village. Benjie and Taylor adored sushi and the restaurant's top cocktail, the "Sambatini." Both were lost on Reese. He believed he was the lone gay man in Manhattan who didn't live for the ingesting of raw fish into his system at the endless opportunities that flooded the City. He hated sushi, not only for its slimy texture, but also for the parasites and bacteria, which roamed throughout its raw flesh. "I'm not going to eat steak tartar, so why should I eat this crap."

But Reese had to bust a move and get uptown to change clothes and then back down again all the while trying to figure out a topic for his weekly column. This was now the fifth consecutive week he was going to be late with his copy. His editor was none too pleased when Reese reached him at the office the night before. "Reese, it's no big deal because your copy is usually tight and needs little work. But you've got to work with me and respect the deadlines I give you."

He tried to play it off but had become disturbed with the casualty with which he has pushed his writing further down his list of priorities. He had been consumed early on with spending as much time with Matt as humanely possible. But now, he was working just as hard to stay out of the way, yet still remain available nearly at all hours.

In the previous week, after a long night out with some of Heath's friends, Matt called around four in the morning insisting that Reese get in a cab and come see him. Although Reese was happy that Matt called for some action, he knew at those moments it was just all about sex. There wasn't any emotion in those nights. It was just two bodies moving together seeking the desired reaction.

Reese had resigned himself to just get to the off-season with Matt in somewhat more of a positive disposition. If Matt wanted sex at four in the morning, he was going to get it at four in the morning. But these were the events that disturbed Reese the most. The fact that he found himself a hypocrite in the eyes of Taylor and Benjie meant little to him. Reese knew they thought he had sold his soul to sit at the cool kid's table.

But he knew Matt loved him. It was the new rules that disturbed him. Why couldn't Matt see him in public? They wouldn't have to hold hands or kiss. Why did Matt have to put so many limitations on Reese's comings and goings? Reese could behave in a crowd or at a game. Matt had seemed to forget that it was his long-time friend and not his boyfriend who attacked the fanatic at the Garden. Maybe he would loosen up after making the playoffs, he thought as the cab rolled up to his apartment.

It was an unusually warmer day as the sun poked through the clouds. The trees that lined Reese's street were showing the birth of the spring's foliage and 51st Street would be in full bloom in a matter of days. Reese longed for the summer and the ample free time he and Matt could spend together away from the spotlight of the NBA. Surely, Matt would loosen the noose strangling their relationship then.

After he quickly picked up his mail and headed up the stairs to his home, he found his neighbor Sharon leaving her apartment.

"Your phone has been going off all morning," she said with enough sleep in her eyes to wipe out a ward full of insomniacs at St. Clare's Hospital. "I tried to get a quick nap in before returning to the spa. There was a water mane break last night that flooded the place."

Looking at his neighbor with guilt, he noticed that her usual voluptuous frame seemed beaten down. Sharon had left a very profitable career as a divorce lawyer to open her own spa in the West Village. "I'm so sorry. I don't know who it could have been. Everyone has my cell number and I've gotten no calls on that."

"It's OK," she said, flashing her brilliant smile. "Where have you been? It seems like I never see you anymore."

"Well, you're always at your spa now," he said, trying not to answer her question. "Are you heading down there now?"

When she responded that she was, he said that he was heading downtown in a few minutes and would split a cab after a quick shower, shave and redress. Her enthusiasm to lie on his couch and not drag herself off to her "dream" business was evident as she followed him into his apartment.

"Just give me a few minutes to collect myself and we're on our way," he said while shutting the bathroom door and starting the water. He didn't actually think that Sharon heard him as he could hear her deep breathing begin nearly as soon as she stretched out on his sofa and fell asleep.

When he emerged from the now saunalike bathroom, refreshed and ready to tackle his afternoon of gluttony with his friends, Sharon was sitting up and quite alert compared to the state in which he had left her just a moment ago. "Wow, my couch must be good. You were closer to death than consciousness when I left you."

"PooBear, are you fucking NBA Matt Walker?"

The question left Reese stunned and it was apparent from

his silence that her suspicions were true. "How? What?" he muttered as he tried to find the words.

"He just called and left a message on your machine."

Just then Reese hated that he set his answering machine to screen so he could hear the messages as they recorded. "What did he say?"

"Not much except that he was mad you left before he woke up, was sorry that you couldn't come to the game last night and hoped that after the season you two could go away with each other."

Running to the windowsill where his answering machine rested, he saw the red light blinking endlessly. Hitting the play button he learned that there were nearly twenty hang-ups before hearing Matt's soothing voice come from the tiny speaker.

True enough to Sharon's statement, he had left a message expressing his disappointment in Reese's hasty departure, regret about his new rule of not having Reese at his games and ultimately wishing for a summer getaway. It was a mixed bag, Reese thought as he turned to face his neighbor who had just learned his biggest secret.

"You can't tell anyone," he insisted.

"Don't be snarky," she said with her raspy voice from her pack-a-day cigarette habit coming through. "I'm not an idiot. But neither are most of the people in this world, which is truly astonishing."

"Good."

"Plus, I already knew. Matt dated my friend Henry last season until Henry couldn't take it anymore. I just have one question for you."

"What?"

"Why would you ever live your life like that?" she said in a tone that was more condemning than inquisitive. She continued to recount her friend's affair with Matt and how Matt had seemed so wonderful at first, but then started applying all these rules of conduct. "Matt would have him out on the town with him at his gallery or at dinner and even at the games, but the bastard wouldn't acknowledge Henry at all. That is until they were alone and Matt just wanted to fuck his ass. He's still in therapy over the way Matt taught him to hate who he is."

"That's not what's going on with me."

"Don't get all-battered-wife syndrome on my ass. Matt Walker will try to change you."

"Honestly, he hasn't," he lied.

"Has he asked you to go out and then proceeded to hide from you all night?" she asked as if she was back in court, litigating a spouse that had done wrong by her client.

"Yes, but . . ."

"Have you gone to one of his games only to be told not to cheer too hard?"

"Well . . ."

"Same shit. Different guy," she concluded. "He wants all the benefits of being famous, without its downside. It's all a façade. His public persona isn't him. I doubt what you're with is the real him. It's all very insulting."

"It's not that simple," Reese argued. "His job isn't just something that is easy to be out in."

"Not everything has to be easy, Reese. I don't own and operate my own spa because it's easy. I do it because I want to do it. He has options. He just refuses to look at them."

"I've been there, Sharon! I've heard the heckles from the stands while he's on the court, or even on the bench. He's been called 'faggot' and worse. He's been through more humiliation than ninety-nine percent of the boys in Chelsea."

"Being a faggot isn't bad, Reese," she said as a matter of fact. "And the simple fact is that the boys in Chelsea aren't ashamed of who they are. But, Matt Walker is."

Reese sank into his sofa still not realizing that the only scrap covering his damp body towel wrapped around his waist.

"Honey, I love you. But you didn't declare yourself as a proud gay man to live in shame, did you?" she said before giving him a kiss on the forehead. "Everything will be fine. Call your friends. Tell them that you'll be at lunch soon. Don't hide. Be proud."

"Thanks Sharon," he said, thinking that she would be a fine addition to the world of great fag hags like Parker Posey, Madonna and Margaret Cho.

But calling to confirm his attendance at the drunken orgy of gossip at Sushi Samba wasn't on the amended agenda. He loved Benjie and Taylor to death, but their sarcasm and "I told you so" eyes weren't anything that Reese could fend off at this particular moment.

He picked up his cell and pressed his "one-touch dialing" button for Taylor. On the phone's third ring she picked up. "Where in the hell are you, fag? We're on our second round already. You know some people do have to go back to work."

"Exactly. Look, I'm going to have to miss today. Tell Benjie that I'm sorry and will talk to him tomorrow. I can't go out with him tonight, either."

"I know Matt doesn't have practice today," she said in her usually loud and buzzed self. "But you don't have to spend all day with him in bed. Heath is getting off early and you don't see me running over there."

"I'm not with Matt, Tay. I'm just way behind on my column and I need to get it done. I'll talk to you tomorrow."

Pushing the end button Reese's eyes welled with tears.

Chapter Twelve

On page 84 of the *Village Voice* ran Reese's latest column.

*   *   *

Last week I rented *Moulin Rouge.* The surprising thing isn't that I don't own the latest evidence that Baz Luhrmann smokes crack, but where I rented it. Normally I head to my locally owned and operated Video Café. But that night, it was cold. It was wet, and damnit, I didn't want to be cold or wet anymore. So I walked the 200 yards to Blockbuster and not the five blocks to the Mom & Pop shop I adore.

See, I have always been that guy who walks the extra few blocks to support the local establishment without fail. So when I ended up under the neon-saturated roof of Blockbuster, staring at the "Sandra Bullock Crap Trilogy" (*Forces of Crap, Practical Crap* and everyone's favorite *Crap Floats*) that lined the back wall, and the Goobers and Gummy Bears hawked in the obligatory impulse-buy aisle near checkout, I was taken aback. This place is all about empty calories, no nutrition for the intellect or the soul.

Years ago, I don't believe that I walked into the Video Café's single glass door at the corner of 48th Street and Ninth Avenue because I wanted to support the little guy in his fight against Big Brother, although it could have been what sparked my interest. I do appreciate the Moms & Pops of this world 'cause they're like me. They're the outcasts, the underdogs of this world. But I refuse to stay beholden to them for that one reason. So, my loyalty to them for all these years is a practical business decision. They offer me what I want; from the Sundance friendly titles to the latest gay dramas to the occasional pornographic DVD. The Video Café gives me what I need to keep my outsider's edge in this bubblegum existence where Mickey Mouse lives in Times Square and there is a Banana Republic in SoHo.

I always knew this day would come, though. My father told me when I was a child that life is full of choices and compromises. And while deciding where to rent *Moulin Rouge* isn't the decision that I should use to define who and what I'm about, it does show me what path I'm on and can be a clue to where I'm going.

When I recently met a new man, I didn't think I was headed for trouble with my choice in a movie rental outlet. But when he was bewildered by my use of the cute little shop at the far corner and not the sterile and mindless corporate fallout shelter he suggested, I was more than a bit miffed.

The irony is that he didn't see himself as the cute little shop at the far corner. He is a choice that isn't convenient at all. He takes work to love and be with, albeit not for his personality, but for his lifestyle. He is not out of the closet and has no plans to change that fact. While our time is spent completing each other's sentences and exploring each other's minds as well as souls, we do so in the shadows of our two very different worlds.

I always believed that relationships shouldn't be work. They should be the Blockbuster on the corner. I shouldn't have to walk past its neon lights when its cold and wet so I can find the safety of the cute little shop at the far corner. That is a statement I don't want to make in the name of love. So as I continue to debate between having the relationship I want or the man I love, I have to ask will love concur all?

Or maybe his little Mom & Pop shop will make it big? Maybe he will come out of the closet and the cute little shop at the far corner will take off with a record-breaking IPO. Maybe we can move from the shadows and into the light. Maybe we will live happily ever after.

And maybe Sandra Bullock will turn out a movie that I don't have to interject the word 'crap' into the title to make it more appealing.

Chapter Thirteen

Looking on the closed circuit security feed from within his building Reese quickly recognized that it was Matt buzzing his apartment at such a late hour. They hadn't spoken since his column hit the street early the day before. Reese had called and left numerous messages both on Matt's cell and at his apartment with Heath. But they went unanswered.

Taylor had even been recruited to spy on Matt as she spent her fourth consecutive night in the SoHo loft. She reported that he spent his entire time behind his bedroom door only coming out to collect a dinner delivery from the attempt-to-be-swanky restaurant, Mercer Kitchen. "He looked like crap, Reese. Why did you write it and then not tell him you were going to publish it?"

He couldn't answer the question, not to her and not to his boyfriend ascending the staircase just twenty paces from his front door. All he knew was that he sat down and wrote his column without thinking of its consequences or repercussions.

Now stumbling around to find a Listerine breath strip, Reese tripped over his end table, jamming his left pinkie toe along its base. While his mind registered the crushing blow of his toe being pried away from the rest of his foot, it took forever until the sharp sting registered. But the throb of pain did come, coincidentally with the ring of his front door bell.

"What the hell is this?" Matt said angrily while waving a copy of the latest *Voice* in the air. But noticing the tears glowing from Reese's eyes he retreated. "I'm sorry. I didn't mean it like that."

Reese recognized he had Matt's sympathy and if they were going to discuss what he thought they were about to, he didn't want, or hopefully need, that advantage. "I stubbed my toe. I'm fine."

"Oh."

"So, I take it that you've read it," Reese said while noticing an affirmative headshake from his boyfriend. "Well, come on in."

The pair walked further into Reese's home as the columnist tried to think of what to say. Finally, he was able to declare that he was scared. "Things have been going so well for us, but when I realized that I was regressing from who I was, I panicked. I know I should have called you or something, but I honestly don't think that I incriminated you at all. There was no mention of you being a professional athlete or any clue at all. For all the average reader knows, you're an investment banker. I didn't Brendan Lemon your ass."

"Although, all the guys on the team will suspect it's me. That's not what concerns me the most, Reese," Matt said, sitting down after collecting a bottle of water from Reese's deserted refrigerator. "The problem is that it reads like you're looking to get out of this relationship 'cause it's not your ideal."

"It's not my ideal, Matt," he said as he took a seat on his sofa, hoping that Matt would choose to sit alongside him and not in the chair along the opposite wall. "It's the furthest thing from it. I can only show you affection when you allow me to touch you. I can only do things with your permission."

"Reese, I love you and I want to see you as much as possible," he said by answering his boyfriend's wish and cozying up to him on the couch. "But in my world, I have to be smart. I don't have that freedom. I honestly want this to work . . ."

"So do I."

"But, we have to remain with the status quo. There are enough rumors about me already. Thank God, you're not coming to any more of my games."

Matt rolled his head back and pinched the bridge of his nose with his index finger and thumb of his right hand. It was obvious to Reese that he wasn't feeling well. Matt looked as he did that morning weeks earlier when he received a call from Ira about the fight at the Garden. Reese didn't want to add to his problems, but he wanted to address the issue that the two men had worked so carefully to avoid.

"I can empathize with the pressure that you're under and I don't want to contribute to it, but a relationship is a two-way street," Reese said. "You've got to give me something to work with. Can't I go back to the Garden? We did go to high school together. We can spin it that we're long-time friends."

"Since Heath's fight died down, you could have returned, I guess. But now, you've written that column. The gossip pages don't need much more than that to dig their claws into. The sad fact is that I can't see you in public, at least not for a while."

Reese took a deep breath while he rubbed his throbbing toe. He didn't want to have this fight. Not with Matt. He truly loved this man, but the price of this love seemed to cost too much.

"I don't live in a world where I'm allowed to be the way that I want to be, or even the way that I am," Matt explained. "It's a compromise I made a long time ago when I decided to be a ballplayer. I resigned myself to live in the locker room, and later I agreed to be in the public eye when I became a professional. Both of those worlds don't play by normal rules."

"You know, before I dated you I thought you were another Tom Cruise or Mike Piazza. Like, where all the fags in the world got together and decided that these men are gay, even if there was no proof of it. Unfortunately for us they seem not to be. But I believe now that if those men did come out, it wouldn't be that big of a deal."

"It's a difficult tight rope for them—and me," Matt said. "When they were accused of being gay, they had to defend their 'straightness' all the while saying it wasn't a bad thing to be gay. You have to be so goddamn politically correct now. Like it's their fault they like pussy. But, my thing is completely different yet played out with similar tactics. I have to make the exact same statements, all the while keeping my real life as private as possible. Cruise, Piazza and all of them at least get to live their real lives in the open. I always thought my situation was closest to Rosie O'Donnell's, but she is a lesbian. We all know that lesbians play by different rules."

"You think they do? The WNBA seems to love the sisters."

"Totally. By a majority of the public, lesbians are seen as a stage of development or something a girl can just fall into. We're the freaks, the sick ones for fucking each other in the ass."

"But the WNBA markets to the lesbian community," Reese argued.

"That's the hypocrisy," Matt countered. "In their players' contracts, the League has ordered the players to portray a wholesome All-American family image on and off the court. The WNBA wants lesbians to buy tickets and merchandise, but they don't want them on the court."

Reese contemplated his next move while he watched Matt sink further into the sofa. Matt had taken Reese's wounded foot and was now affectionately massaging its damaged appendage.

"Oww, that hurts!" Reese exclaimed as he pulled his foot away from Matt.

"It could be broken."

"Doubt it," he said in a dismissive manner. "But back to the discussion. I'm having a hard time accepting that the League would act in such an obtuse way. I mean, we've come a long way in integrating ourselves into pop culture. My column and all the sitcoms blasting into every home in Iowa have helped educate and expose our lives to people who are normally repulsed by it."

"Your column doesn't cross the Hudson," Matt said as he rolled his eyes in contempt and hoped that this discussion would disappear. Why did all the men he date have to bring up 'coming out' in their fifth week together? For as much as gay men were notorious for being late or on 'gay time,' they were never late with this topic. "And as far as those sitcoms go, do you really think a flaming queen with their drunken rich girlfriend is making a difference to the farmers of America?"

"You can't say that it's not making a difference. Just the simple fact that it's on is a degree of success. By being out in the public eye, we're educating them. Plus, the acceptance of gay issues in our media shows an acceptance among advertisers who pay for the programming. And God knows they don't do anything unless it's going to help their bottom line."

"Come on, Reese. These people would still tie you up to a fence post in Wyoming and leave you for dead."

"Me? Yes." Reese conceded. "But you? Never. They would see you as one of them. It's people like you who would make a bigger difference."

"I am not a role model and it shouldn't be argued that I am one," Matt said dryly. "I am an anonymous athlete. People who watch my games do not know who I am and they don't give a damn about me unless I can put a ball through a hoop."

"Of course they don't know the real you. You haven't given them a chance to know you. Hell, you haven't given anyone a chance to know you, the real you."

"I am not just a gay man," Matt said with a bit more authority in his voice. Meeting Reese's eyes with his own, he continued. "I'm sick and tired of the gay agenda and its belief that all public people should advertise their sexuality. I just want to play ball while I can. I don't see a reason to rock the boat when I have such a limited time to take advantage of the opportunities that I have worked so hard to get."

"But it's not just about you. When I came out the only thing it did was perpetuate the myth of what a gay man is. No one noticed or was surprised. It would be different with you though!"

"Yeah, it would be different. Like you said, nothing happened to you. And you're right; it's not exactly unusual for an NYU boy to be gay. It would ruin me."

"I don't think that's how things would be anymore. Especially here in New York. Everyone in this city knows someone who is gay. I don't think people would really even think twice about it."

"Come on Reese, I know you are not this stupid, but I didn't think you were this naïve. Most of these so-called enlightened people you are talking about are people like your friends, not people who pay hundreds of dollars a night to watch the NBA. And I know for damn sure that none of those people are the type who would be progressive enough to buy my jersey or my shoe if I ever got a shoe deal after coming out."

"Does anyone actually still buy jerseys anyways? I thought that was a horrible side-effect of the popularity of hip-hop in the mid-nineties."

"You've just proven my point!" Matt exclaimed, growing more frustrated with Reese. "Yes, people still buy merchandise. Do you have any idea how important it is to be the type of player who can move merchandise? Even if every gay person in America came to my aid, I don't think they'd allow themselves to buy the latest Nike jersey or shoe."

"Well, if it was Adidas or Puma they would. Those are always popular with the faux-butch Chelsea gym fags." Reese quipped, trying to lighten the mood.

"That's not the fucking point!" Matt yelled as he hurled one of the sofa's numerous pillows against the opposite wall.

"Geez, calm down babe. I'm only messing with you."

"I know. I'm sorry. It's just that I've had to listen to this argument so many times my entire life," Matt said as he lowered his head. Finally, in a near whimper he asked, "Don't you think that I realize how it could help some people?"

"Then why not do it? I think I know you pretty well, and I seriously doubt some potential merchandising deals are enough to outweigh the possibility of truly helping, even saving, some people."

"It's not that simple. You're assuming that my teammates, coaches and management would be fine with everything. Unless I miraculously got good enough that I could win games on my own, everything still comes down to team chemistry. It's a giant leap of faith to assume that no one in that locker room wouldn't be bothered by my slapping them on the ass, as if it would have meant anything more than a job well done."

"Don't you see, the barrier has to be broken for the issue to go away? Nowadays no one notices what color the guy who plays centerfield for the Yankees is, but fifty years ago it was a big deal," Reese reasoned before continuing. "But, if someone who plays a sport that is dominated by minorities, in a city known for its diversity and tolerance, has a problem with someone being gay, it's their fucking problem."

"It becomes my fucking problem when apparent minor comments or jokes about it accompany, directly or coincidentally with a drop in team performance or attendance. Then it's no longer about some homophobic bigot, it's about ticket sales, the playoffs, championship rings. Even with megastars like Michael and Kobe, this sport is still about television deals and winning. There are going to be certain markets, say Memphis or Utah where people won't want to watch a team with a faggot on it."

"You're just being ridiculous. Like anyone is going to be worried about losing the support of Jim Bob in Tennessee."

"That's exactly what the guys in the marketing department will be thinking about," Matt argued. "This isn't some little hobby for people with nothing better to do, Reese! This is serious shit. There is an insane amount of money involved in this business. It would be a little hard for me to negotiate a contract at the end of the season, if there were questions about my marketability, regardless of my playing ability."

"So it is all about money for you. I can't fucking believe that you don't even care how much you could help people."

"How is my coming out going to change anything? I'm not that famous. Do you really think some homophobe jock in Wyoming is gonna not care about people being gay anymore because I came out?"

"I think you're seriously underselling yourself Matt. It's quite obvious that a whole helluva lot of straight guys idolize athletes like you, more than their fathers or anyone else. If they found out you were gay maybe they would think twice the next time they were getting ready to bash some poor gay boy. If they . . ."

"I don't think that's the type of connection they'd be making. It wouldn't really help if I didn't get to play anymore. It's a great example to show, be gay lose your . . ."

"Can I please finish? If they had the opportunity to see that someone who was playing ball was gay, and was quasi-normal. It would stand to argue that being gay is normal, too. Maybe nobody else would have to be tied to a fence post."

"Fuck off! Don't give me that. That is so damn wrong of you!"

"What? It's the truth!"

"You're saying because I didn't come out, that's why Matthew was killed. That's some fucked up shit Reese!"

"That's not what I'm saying at all. No one is to blame for that except for those two fuckheads. I'm just saying, maybe some big star coming out is the first step in making sure nothing like that ever happens again."

"The first step is having parents teach their kids not to kill each other," Matt said. Again pinching the bridge of his nose, he continued. "OK, look. I obviously don't want anyone to get beaten to death, or even harassed because of who they are. But it just doesn't seem fair, right, or realistic for me to risk everything I've worked for my entire life for the chance that it would change anything. This is my dream, Reese. I've wanted what I now have for as long as I can remember. Why should I risk it? Why is it my responsibility?"

"'Cause change just doesn't happen randomly. People have to fight for it. Progress isn't free. Someone has to pay the price, and unfortunately for you, you can afford it."

"Remember who you are talking to for a second. Don't you think that I know all of this? I'm not a stupid jock who happens to be gay. I went to Stanford and graduated with honors. I'm cultured and aware of my place in the world, so I can grasp the concept of social change. But again, why does it have to be me? Trust me on this one, there are other guys in the League, and in other sports who could do it just as well as I could. Why should I be the one who has to subject himself to the crap shouted from the stands, the hate mail, the death threats and the animosity from coaches and management? And don't think for one second that all my teammates will be as cool as Wayne about this."

"Come on, your teammates . . ."

"Oh, they're just as backwards as the rest of the world." Matt spat out. "You can't argue that professional teams are a microcosm of society by saying there are gay men amongst its ranks and not accept that they're homophobes and bigots too. Take that bitch on the Grizzlies. He found some fans sitting courtside annoying so he started shouting shit at them, including those all-too-popular anti-gay catch phrases."

"But what if this is what you're supposed to do? What if this is why you were born? Why you're good at basketball? Why you ended up playing in the largest media market in the world? Maybe this is your story."

"Jesus Christ, don't go all 'this is your birthright' on me. I'm not 'Matty The Homophobe Slayer.'"

"Oh wow. The weapons would be so cool if you were like 'Buffy Part Two,' though I don't think I could handle the breasts and the 'sand monster.'" Reese said laughing at his own joke. Luckily, Matt found it rather amusing as well and was laughing along with him.

"Look, all I'm saying is that you're like the perfect person to do this. You're smart, articulate and look like the All-American boy."

"That's fine and all, it's your opinion, but it's my decision. You may be quite gracious for thinking about the solitary gay boy in Nebraska, but it affects my life most directly, and that should be my only concern. No one else puts food on my table."

Chapter Fourteen

"Hey fool, what are you up to?" chimed an overly chipper Benjie as soon as Reese had removed the cordless phone from its base.

"Hey queen, nothing much, just sitting around, watching the *Girls* on TiVo from earlier when I was at the gym."

"Oh my God, the seven or the seven-thirty episode? The seven was the funniest episode ever. You know, I've seen everyone of them like a thousand times, but this one still makes me completely lose it. Rose is just so ridiculous."

"Benjie, you know I love Rose, I am Rose. But Sophia is the funniest part of the show. I love her calling Blanche a whore, floozy, and Blanche loves her for it. It's kind of how our relationship works."

"Whatever, Rose makes me laugh my ass off. So, you got any plans?"

"I was gonna work on my column. Watch some TV, maybe go get a DVD for later, since invariably there will be nothing on my 285 channels. Digital cable is fucking fantastic!" Reese explained sarcastically.

"You're such a loser, Reese! It's Friday night, and I haven't seen you in like two weeks. I need to go out. We haven't given the boys at the lounges about town a looksie in months. You have to be wantin' some lovin'. God knows I am."

"Benjie, have I been blessed by the God I don't believe in? Do you remember the little secret we discussed at lunch?"

"Of course I remember. I've been working on getting an interview with the gayest of all the Knicks for next week."

"Benjie!"

"Unhitch your panties. You know I'm fucking with you. Listen. Just come out with me. Maybe you'll meet someone. Maybe you won't. But don't take yourself off the market for some guy who you can't even hold hands with at the movies. There's no way it's gonna last anyway."

"Thanks for the vote of confidence. But Blanche, err Benjie, I just don't feel like going out. I have to get this column done."

"Lame! You are so goddamn lame," Benjie squealed, not believing that his wingman had turned into a perpetual nester. "I know when your column is due, and I know you don't work on it at all on Friday nights. I am getting you back out on the market if it kills me. You better be at my place by eleven or I will personally send one of those sleazy escorts, advertised in the back of one of those gay rags, over to your place with an assortment of whips and chains. Your choice!" Benjie said with a maniacal laugh as he hung up the phone.

"Fuck!" Reese said out loud as he evaluated the seriousness of Benjie's threat. Whenever Benjie really wanted to go out and find some boys, there was usually very little that could be done to stop him. There was no way that Benjie was going to let the weak excuse of doing work that Reese had given persuade him to stay in. So Reese, glancing at the clock and noticing he had about forty minutes, quickly shaved and put on an outfit he thought wouldn't attract too much attention.

As he exited his building and walked towards the "C" subway stop at 50th Street, Reese decided that he didn't feel like riding in what would most certainly be a subway packed tightly with people on their way to getting sauced, and some people who were already there. He hadn't really been able to tolerate any sort of crowd since the melee at the Knick game. Reese wasn't sure if it was just the trauma of the event, or if the feeling of anxiety he was experiencing was connected to the tension that had developed in his relationship with Matt.

After telling the cab driver to aim for the intersection of Jane and Hudson, Reese thought about what was happening between

Matt and himself. Reese desperately wanted Matt to come out of the closet, but he concluded that it wasn't a deal breaker. But thankfully due to the other night, Reese felt comfortable with the manner in which the topic was dealt. He didn't issue an ultimatum or make over-the-top statements in an attempt to steal the argument. So Reese was pretty sure that they had survived their first major fight, although the subject had not been spoken of again. The tension was palpable.

As the cab approached Benjie's corner, Reese decided to accept Heath's explanation about the change in Matt's demeanor. He said his roommate was under a lot of pressure now that the Knicks were only two games away from clinching a birth in the playoffs. And while there were no more reports from the gossip pages making veiled references to a Knick whose sexuality wasn't too clear, the sports pages and radio call-in shows were another entity all to themselves. There were reports in the sports pages about "troubling rumors" distracting the players, and on the radio fans called to put in their two cents of how "that guard's sexuality" was bad for team morale.

Finding Benjie waiting impatiently at his corner, Reese paid the driver quickly not worrying about the extra large tip he gave. "You are so lucky that you decided to come." Benjie said as he showed Reese which of the escorts that would have been heading to the Hell's Kitchen apartment if Reese didn't make his presence felt.

"Why in God's name did you pick him? He looks like a cracked-out gorilla! Of course, the ten-by-seven-inch measurement seems like a marvelous challenge."

"I'm sure those are *gay* inches," Benjie quipped in a stab at most fags who added an inch or two to their member's measurement. "But, that is exactly the point. If you hadn't shown, I wasn't about to give you a hot boy as a reward for staying home on a Friday night. Those will be what we find over some drinks."

"So, we going to Hell?" Reese asked even though he could tell that was their destination from the westward direction in which they had started walking.

"I figured why not? I mean it's right there."

"True. I mean the East Village does have the hotter crowd on a Friday, but I always love the fact that while you love cock, you choose convenient cock over cross-town cock. Do you hate the subway that much?" Reese asked rhetorically before changing directions. "So, what's been up with you? How's work?"

"Work is work. My boss is a total ass. So, I've been spending a lot of time at the gym, trying to blow off steam. That's pretty much what I do when I'm not at work."

"I didn't know that giving blow jobs in the steam room made your arms explode," Reese said dryly. "I mean, Benjie! Your guns are getting huge."

"Well, let's just say that I have a new interest in staying at the gym longer."

"Who is it now?" Reese asked eagerly. He was glad that he was hearing the story early enough into one of Benjie's crushes that he could hear about the excitement and not the stage when he would inevitably say, "Oh, he took more than ten minutes from when I came to get out of bed and leave."

"He is so fucking hot, Reese. You can't help but look at him," Benjie said as they walked through Hell's bordello red doors. The pair had always been particularly fond of this watering hole, partly because of the kitschy 1960s and '70s television stars who were immortalized with drawn red horns and moustaches on their black and white photographs that clung to the walls.

"I met him before—somewhere on Fire Island, I think. I've taken to calling him 'The Protagonist,'" Benjie said cheerfully. He continued raving that his friend Josh and he had met 'The Protagonist' at a tea dance the previous summer, but hadn't hit it off. Apparently, they still hadn't hit it off, but that wasn't going to stop Benjie, since he was now interested. "He's so hot, he just can't be referred to by name. He's the one who makes everything OK. Everyone else loves the name—The Protagonist. Isn't it perfect? Cause he's the hero in the story!"

"Oh come on, he can't . . . ," started Reese before noticing the most perfect example of "dirty hot" walking through the lounge's double doors. His long dark hair was more than disheveled as he strolled up to the bar ten feet down from the two friends with their respective jaws dropped. Dirty Hot wore a Decepticon t-shirt and dangerously low cut jeans exposing a perfectly taught lower stomach. It was a stomach that hadn't been overworked in the gym, just toned from hours of sex and cigarettes. While Reese wasn't a big fan of the two-day stubble, the not-so-clean-shaven look worked extremely well on Dirty Hot.

"Damn!" Benjie exclaimed failing to hold back his excitement. "Smack my ass and order him a drink, Reese. What a delicious cocktail he would be!"

Finding a clear spot along the bar now within eyesight of his new prey, Benjie waved down the bartender with a trendy faux-hawk and a sprinkling of tattoos along his upper arms. "What can I get for ya?" the bartender asked, already setting up a couple glasses with ice.

"How 'bout an intro with that devil?" Benjie asked while nodding his head toward Dirty Hot. "But if he *or you* aren't interested, I'll take the house cocktail, a wicked bitch. I'm sure this one will require a Maker's Manhattan, up, heavy on the vermouth."

As the bartender got to work, quickly making the drinks, Benjie turned his back to the bar and did a speedy assessment of the potential tricks lounging around the place, making certain to catch the eye of his Decepticon.

"There are too many women here on Friday night," Benjie said in disgust. "So, 'The Protagonist' lives just around the corner from here. I wonder if he cruises here often."

"How do you know where he lives?"

"I followed him home from the gym one afternoon," Benjie said as a matter of fact.

"Stalker!"

"I don't have a problem with it."

"I'm sure *he* does."

"How will he ever find out?" Benjie asked. "It's not like you're going to say anything. I've got the goods on your ass."

Reese rolled his eyes as he heard Benjie continue to explain how he simply wanted to know more about his man so he could play the odds of running into him in more places than just the gym. "If he goes to a particular grocery, I should be there. If he goes to a particular dry cleaner, I should use it. See, little Reese, this is how single girls get their man."

Benjie handed the bartender a twenty, tipping him a dollar for each drink, and handed Reese his Manhattan.

"Look, that couch just opened up. Let's grab it!" Reese demanded as he swiftly walked away so Benjie couldn't object. Benjie always wanted to stand in high-traffic areas at bars so that he would have the chance to cop a feel, be felt up, or at least make eye contact with a potential hook up. Benjie thought he was way too pretty to ever not be on Center Stage.

"Why the fuck are we sitting down over here in the corner?" Benjie asked in disgust as he saddle up alongside Reese in the lounge's far corner. "There was a forty-year-old who was beside you that wasn't totally far from decent. He was checking both of us out, and judging by what he was wearing, we could have scored some free drinks off of him. Did you see the Beluga watch?"

"I don't feel like standing up all night," Reese said with contempt for being dragged out on the town. He was now sure that the night would get increasingly painful as he was forced to witness Benjie creep ever closer to senility. "Here we have a waiter to bring us drinks. And you know I feel dirty playing some old man just to get free drinks for the night."

"It's how the game is played," Benjie said in his most authoritative manner. "We're younger, he's richer. He buys us drinks and we give him some eye candy. And if he's lucky, he might get the home version of the game as well."

"That isn't how it has to be. Do you really think you're going to find anything successful with a guy from a bar? Plus, the times I've gone out with the intention of meeting someone or taking someone home, I only seem to catch someone significantly weirder, or significantly fatter."

"Oh listen to you! You're in a six-week . . ."

"Seven."

"Whatever. Seven-week relationship with a closeted man," Benjie said. "Don't get all holier than thou on my ass. The simple fact is that you don't have any clue on what you're doing when you enter a bar. The first rule is that you never sit in the corner like this. You have to be up and have your ass accessible for the grabs and rubs that will surely come. Second, you never wear anything from last season, let alone this little get-up you have from *three years ago*. And finally, you're here for cock, Reese. You're not here to find someone to run off and open a bed and breakfast with in Vermont."

"I know the rules, thank you. I just don't feel like it. I don't want to meet someone that way; think about how it sounds if it does turn into something real. People ask you where you met, and in year twenty-five you're still saying, 'well, we were at a bar and he happened to grab my ass right when I grabbed his crotch.' That sounds perfect for a golden anniversary party."

"You are such a breeder in gay clothing. Why are you worried about having an anniversary," Benjie began but suddenly leaped upon Reese, blocking his view of the bar, "Holy Shit! Look who just came in!"

"I could if you weren't up in my face. Move!" Reese demanded.

"I don't know if you're going to like it," Benjie cooed before finally saying, "It's Adam."

When Benjie slid off Reese, he saw his ex-boyfriend for the first time since their disastrous breakup. He looked good. But as he saw Adam recognize his presence, Reese's chest began to tighten and his breath came in short supply.

"Damn, he looks good," Reese said with a hint of lust in his voice.

"Too good," Benjie quipped. "Botox?"

Ignoring his friend's jaded and bitter comment, Reese watched as Adam moved his way across the crowded floor towards him. Adam was shorter than Reese, but had always carried himself better so he always appeared to be the taller of the two men. His luxurious black hair now eclipsed his jaw line accentuating his sharp facial features while his chest, which always had been a strength, seemed larger and now matched his hulking shoulders.

"Hello Reese, long time no talk. How are you doing?" Adam asked in his deep burley voice.

"I'm fine, Adam. How are you?" Reese said in a lame attempt to act like he wasn't interested in seeing or talking to him.

"I'm good, thank you," Adam continued in his very familiar formal fashion. "How are you Benjamin?"

"I'm fine," Benjie said as he rose from his seated position. "I'm heading over there. Hope to see you boys in the not-so-near future!"

Adam quickly grabbed Benjie's deserted location and grabbed the attention of a passing cocktail boy. Reese could have killed Benjie for abandoning him with his ex-boyfriend, but he knew it would make no difference. Benjie had come into the bar with Reese and was intent on leaving it with another man.

"So, what the hell are you doing here?" Reese asked. "I thought you hated this place."

"I never said that. I just hated coming here with you," Adam answered while gathering his drink and another Manhattan he ordered for Reese. Reese noticed Adam waved off a tip when he placed two twenties in the cocktailer's hand. "Remember us later."

"But let's set the record straight, Reese," he continued. "You became too possessive of me whenever we went out because I ran into so many people that I knew."

"You mean people you *fucked*."

Not nibbling on Reese's bait, Adam said, "I just didn't feel like giving you any more reasons to be suspicious of me. Sometimes I felt like I was dating the CIA."

"Don't think I didn't have good reason to be suspicious of you. You were fucking half of Chelsea," Reese said as he noticed Benjie had already garnered the attention of Dirty Hot. Benjie would be out the door in less than ten minutes.

"I don't know who you've been talking to, but I was not sleeping with half of Chelsea. Hell, I've maybe slept with three guys from Chelsea my entire time in New York."

"Technicalities," Reese answered with little desire to pursue the topic further. "But, I have my sources and a bad case of crabs for about a month after we broke up. They were such the nice parting gift. Thank you, Adam."

"I didn't think I got those till afterwards," Adam giggled. "I'm truly sorry."

"It's fine now . . . but I do get to call you 'The Bastard' for the rest of my life."

"If that's what you have to do, fine," Adam said in resolution. "But, honestly, I didn't sleep around on you that much. For the record, I had no intention of fucking that guy on New Year's. I was just tweaked out of my mind. I was flying. All I wanted to do was fuck, and you weren't there."

"God forbid, if I wasn't around when your cock wanted to burrow in someone's ass!" Reese shrieked in horror. "It's called self-control, Adam. What the hell is your problem?"

"My problem?" Adam asked as the two men's voices began to build in volume. "You honestly don't remember, do you? You have to make me the bad guy in this and not see my fucking other men as a symptom of our twisted relationship!"

"What are you talking about?" a bewildered Reese asked with crossed eyes and shriveled mouth. Throughout their entire relationship, Reese doubted many of Adam's excuses when he had to explain why he couldn't go out on a night when he was not suppose to wait tables, or when he came home late, looking like he had just come from the gym. "I was running late, so I ran. You know how hot it is outside."

"You never thought that all those accusations you made never became a self-fulfilling prophecy," Adam said in a lower voice since they had become acutely aware of the audience the two had attracted. "I got to a point where I thought, I'm damned if I don't fuck around and damned if I do! Choosing between those two options, I chose the latter."

"If your lies didn't suck ass, maybe you wouldn't have felt forced to do the same," Reese snarked.

"Reese it was only sex, it wasn't love. They are two different things."

"Bullshit."

"Can this be water under the bridge? I'm very sorry. I didn't mean to hurt or embarrass you in any way."

"Why should I believe any of this? Why are you even bothering to apologize?"

"I'm trying to apologize because you never let me. You wouldn't return my calls. You wouldn't even respond to e-mails. All I wanted to do was explain the situation and, hopefully, not have you hate me for the rest of your life."

"Oh, I was only going to hate you for the rest of your life." Reese smirked while trying to maintain his bitterness so that he wouldn't give into Adam's charms.

"Damnit! If every gay guy hated their past boyfriends who cheated on them as much as you seem to, we'd be a much more violent people."

"Yes, I hate you. I think I have the right to. I guess eventually I'll get over it, but I'm nowhere near that point," Reese said, trying to lay the guilt on as thick as possible.

"Listen, I'm tired of this and of this scene," Adam said while letting out a deep breath as if he was giving up. "You've obviously had a lot to drink. Do you want to go down to Florent, get some grub, and talk a little more? Think of it as a peace offering on my behalf."

"Well, I'd have to check with Benjie," Reese said as he scanned the room in hopes of finding a reason to avoid more time with Adam. But Reese discovered that Benjie had succeeded in his mission and had Dirty Hot's arms draped around Benjie's tiny waist. It appeared Benjie's target had fallen for the well-developed triceps and biceps busting through his pseudo 1984 Rugby shirt.

Turning back to Adam, already having decided to not be a complete ass, Reese looked at him, nodded, and stood up. "OK, let's go. I could use some food."

Having made their way through what had become an extremely crowded bar, the pair of old lovers stepped out onto the sidewalk, and quickly walked down to the upscale diner at the end of the block. Since it was a very short walk, the alcohol shielded them from the biting cold of the night that was described as winter's last gasp.

In another amazing stroke of luck, the pair was immediately escorted to a lonely two-top in the back of the restaurant. Walking past the bar, both Reese and Adam made sure to take notice of whom they would be dining with that nippy night. It had always been reported in the gossip columns that many famous New Yorkers and visitors frequented the diner for its down and out hipster mentality and its over-the-top wait staff.

The two sat in a loaded, awkward silence while they examined the menus. Fortunately, in Adam's opinion, yet annoying to Reese, the discomfort was broken by their mutual laughter at the antics of the particularly lively waiter. What was obviously one of his favorite songs, Madonna's "Borderline," had cycled onto the restaurant's sound system, and after pumping up the volume, he proceeded to encourage many of the patrons to dance along as he vogued through the restaurant, taking orders and dropping off drinks.

"What's it gonna be baby?" asked the lively waiter named Lester.

"I'll have the grilled cheese sandwich," Reese said, "and a big glass of water."

"And what can I get you sexy?" Lester asked Adam, staring him up and down with a huge smile, showing his overly bleached teeth.

"I'll have the grilled chicken salad with the vinaigrette on the side and a diet coke," Adam said as he enjoyed Lester's attention of placing his hand snuggly on the middle of Adam's back.

Reese was quick to notice the waiter's flirtation, as well as Adam's unusual order. When they had dated, Reese had always had to endure Adam's lectures about how he hated how every fag in the City considered salads to be actual meals. Adam had preferred cheese-laden sandwiches and burgers to the traditional gay fare. Considering this change, as well as the waiter's blatant attraction to Adam, Reese became more aware of how much his ex's appearance had changed since their breakup. While always quite proper and put together, Reese saw that Adam's somewhat rougher edges had been smoothed over. His hair was glowing, as was his skin. He wore a better style of clothing to accentuate his shrinking waistline.

"You're ordering a salad?" Reese asked not knowing if laughter was a proper addendum to the question.

"Yes, I've changed my whole routine," he said without a trace of pride or arrogance. "Once I got the Miller Lite Super Bowl commercial, right after we broke up, I decided I needed to up the ante and raise my stock. Not only do I look a lot better, I just feel better? I don't drink as much. I quit smoking, both pot and cigarettes. I just have so much more extra energy. I love it."

"That's great. Good for you," Reese said as he began to see Adam in a fresh light. He thought that maybe Adam's insides had transformed as much as his façade, and before Reese could stop himself he asked, "You seeing anyone?"

"A few people, but nothing serious. I haven't had time for more. It's just sex and just enough to keep the pipes from backing up."

"So nothing really has changed then," Reese said as his tone turned bitter once again.

"Damnit, Reese," Adam cried. "What's the big deal? Yes, I fucked around! Yes, I wasn't completely honest! Yes, it's my entire fault! Is that what you want to hear?"

Reese sat there stunned, waiting for something to come to him. But when neither the food nor a quick jibe did, Adam continued, "You have to let some things go. We weren't good for each other because you wanted me to be someone who I wasn't or couldn't be."

"We got some live ones here Tina!" Lester shouted to a girl behind the counter. "You boys don't get too rowdy, else I'll have to take one of you out back, so you can put it in my backside," he said, slapping Adam on his chest before walking away, sashaying his hips from side to side.

"I think someone has an admirer," smirked Reese, thankful for the interruption. He didn't feel the need to argue with Adam anymore. He finally felt the type of closure he believed he needed.

"Yeah right. He's just being a smart waiter. Stuff like that always raises the tips from the gay boys." Adam replied while showing off his newly brightened smile.

"I know I was an utter asshole, but why did we completely stop talking?" asked a suddenly more optimistic Adam.

"Well, after starting my New Year with your big bang, I just decided that it would be easier and less painful if we never spoke again," Reese said coldly, almost as if he was talking about the weather. "You know my issues with trust. It's a Catch-22. I always believe the best about people, but once they lose that trust it's hard for them to get it back. Walking into the loft and seeing you lighting your sparkler in that twink's ass . . . well, you pretty much lost all my trust with that thrust."

"I never expected you to forgive me anytime soon after that, but I didn't think you'd never talk to me again," Adam said, hoping that he could bridge the gap between the two men once again. "While we both know that we're no good together as boyfriends, why don't we try it as friends?"

Reese smiled to himself, wondering if he could trust him as a friend or if the betrayal was too big to overcome. He honestly missed very little about Adam. He was a self-absorbed prat, who could easily say one thing and mean quite another. Reese already had Benjie, which was enough for him.

But Adam seemed sincere and there was a change in his eyes and in his tone of voice. While Adam was a fine actor, he was never this good. A problem with dating an actor, Reese believed, was that most actors don't know who they are. So they play a role defined by their boyfriend's interest and needs. It's the casting couch syndrome. "I will become whatever you want be to be, as long as I get the part," these types think to themselves.

Combine that with Reese's desire for a sweet, honest, mature boyfriend. It was an unfortunate miscast for Adam from the beginning.

"Sure, we can be friends," Reese lied. "I don't see the harm in that."

"Excellent!" Adam said, finishing his salad and knocking back the rest of his diet coke. "So then tell me all about this boy you wrote about in your column. Is he an actor?"

Reese laughed out loud as he finally found the trick Adam was trying to turn. He wanted gossip. It explained why Adam approached him at Hell. It was the reason why Adam was quick to accept all the blame for their relationship. This explained everything.

"You know you're as good of an actor as you think you are," Reese said while slapping a ten dollar bill down and putting on his jacket. "It's been a blast, Adam. Really, we shouldn't do this again."

"Oh get off of it!" Adam yelled as Reese began to walk away. "Just remember to make this guy into someone who he ain't just to fulfill your own twisted desires! That works for you every time!"

Walking towards the subway, feeling the buzz drain away from his head, Reese recalled his relationship with Adam up until New Year's Eve. The two had never been that close—emotionally speaking. They only really connected between the sheets. They weren't the type of couple their friends loved to be around. Many would come up with the lamest excuses to avoid their dinner parties and weekend excursions to Vermont or the shore. They had never enjoyed the looks of envy from other gay boys as they walked down the sidewalk holding hands. They were always very uncomfortable together.

Now pulling his jacket around his face to lessen the chill of the howling New York wind, Reese cursed the bitter cold. He approached the 14th Street subway entrance, still thinking about how shallow and deceptive Adam had been before thinking about the ongoing tension with Matt. Reese hadn't made Matt into anyone he wasn't, had he? Definitely not. If anything, he thought, Matt was making him into something Reese Gibbons wasn't.

Chapter Fifteen

Reese was rattled out of sleep by his usual unofficial alarm clock, the banging metal gates being raised at the German restaurant across the street. Most days Reese was thankful to live across from the "Wurst Restaurant" in the City. It always smelled good, had good authentic Bavarian beer, and never stayed open late enough to keep him awake on the rare evenings that he went to bed before midnight. This morning, however, still reeling from numerous drinks with Benjie and an intense conversation with Adam, Reese awoke, cursing the Germans in his best French accent.

"Aww, Tse fooking Germans, Why arree Tse avays tso lowd."

Before he could fully indulge himself in one of his favorite pastime, mocking the French, Reese remembered that he had setup a running date with one of his marathon training partners. Reese had never really given up running from his days at the Academy. During college he had slacked off a bit, which he justified as a necessary break from the constant training of his high school years. Once he finished school and settled into his New York gay lifestyle, Reese became acutely aware of how necessary it was to stay in shape. This realization resulted in Reese resuming his running workouts, mostly by committing to a friend who was training for the New York City Marathon, a tradition that had continued each subsequent year.

After chomping down an energy bar so he'd have something in his stomach, Reese laced up his running shoes and dashed out of his apartment towards Central Park. It being a Saturday, and Reese still being hungry after the energy bar, the site of everyone doing brunch inside the various Ninth Avenue eateries, made Reese's stomach growl and turn in anger. The post-workout feast would be more than an hour away and his head ached, knowing that fact.

When Reese arrived at the Columbus Circle entrance to the Park, after nearly being killed by an oncoming bus when he meandered into the street, he came upon his editor, David, who was serving as this season's running partner.

Last year's marathon attempt was cut short as Benjie wouldn't commit to running anything over five miles. "Unless Matt Damon is giving out BJs, you will never see me run that far." And so was born his infatuation with growing his arms to near hulkish proportions.

David stood against a lamppost along Park Drive, arms crossed, casually checking out the numerous young runners who were working off the three or four drinks they had had the night before, when he noticed Reese approaching him.

"I thought I was going to get your column before you showed, dickhead," David shouted, catching the attention of a large pack of older ladies strutting their stuff in t-shirts and leotards, "Did you have to kick some young stud out of bed?"

"No, and this week's column is already done thank you very much," Reese lied. "I'm hungover. Can we just get started?"

"See, that's why you gotta get a little action in the morning, it works out all the party residue from the night before," David said as the two began their jog in a counter-clockwise direction around Central Park Drive. "But of course, that was before I got married and had two children."

"Oh yeah, do tell me about the world of David, pre-Emily and the munchkins!" Reese mocked as he stretched out his shoulders, nearly knocking over a young lady who seemed well into her day's journey.

David, a rare Southern California native making a home in New York City, had been one of Reese's most ardent supporters in his personal and private life over the past five years. While just past the age where a heterosexual man advertises his age, the perpetually young at heart David was there for his young and talented writer with advice on sentence structure, as well as men troubles.

The first three miles of the predetermined six-mile route were always devoted to idle chitchat ranging from David's twin girls who had started playing on a peewee soccer team to Reese's shopping sprees on Madison Avenue with Taylor. Around the Harlem tennis courts, David finally broke down and asked what he had been meaning to get out of Reese since its publication. "So, who is this guy you wrote about?"

"I really don't want to talk about it, David."

"Don't or can't?"

"Can't."

"OK, I understand," he said as he tried to pick up his pace with the onset of the Road Runner's Club beginning to pass the duo along the half-mile climb at the Park's most northern point. "But do me one favor, if you can. I really want tickets to the upcoming game versus the Celtics."

"Wha—" Reese said, stopping dead in his tracks, causing numerous runners to take evasive action to avoid a pile up.

"Lucky guess," David said as he shrugged his head and waved Reese on with his left hand.

"Damn, I wish I wasn't such an open book."

"I don't think you are," David said. "But I know your writing more than anyone else in the world and it was evident in how you wrote about him, indirectly of course, in the column about that game system. I could read that you were in awe of something. It just took me another piece or two to figure out what."

"You could tell from that?"

"Actually, no," David conceded. "I just wanted to make myself sound smarter. I have to keep up the image that I'm a quick guy, remember I am the editor of *The Village Voice*. But to be honest, I figured it out when you were involved in that ruckus at the Garden. Then your column spelled it out for me."

Reese began to worry as he counted the number of people

who had learned of his relationship with Matt and prayed that everyone could keep their respective mouths shut.

"I just have one question for you," David said as the two men were negotiating through a much slower running group as they approached the Reservoir. "Does he know about the column that I killed a few years back where you attempted to out every man in Hollywood, Washington, D.C. and any place else a gay man had slept?"

Over the final mile of their workout, Reese tried to argue that while he still believed in his earlier writing, he was trying to amend its hard-line attitude. Of course this wasn't because he actually changed his belief on the issue, he just didn't want to sound like a complete hypocrite to the man who ruled his copy.

"Well, I don't envy your position, Reese," David said as he waved to his wife and kids who ran up to greet their champion. "It's going to be rough if it comes out, which you know, I would love as an exclusive."

Reese laughed at the idea of giving his boyfriend the "honor" of coming out to the *Voice*, but quietly hoped that Matt's coming out day would come sooner rather than later. "It's rough enough already."

"Reese, ready for breakfast?" Emily asked. "Morgan and Mason both want biscuits from the bakery on Amsterdam."

"Oh, that sounds great. But I have plans," Reese lied as he wiped the dirty blond hair from Morgan's eyes. "I hope I can get a rain check."

"Weese, you come ovah an' I show you new biwickle," young Morgan demanded.

"David got the girls new bicycles for the summer," Emily said, rolling her eyes at her husband's ambition. "I think they're too young, but who am I to argue if only their mother?"

Seeing the couple happily on each other's nerves excited Reese in a way that he hadn't expected. The girls' giddiness to see their father, as well as seeing Emily being pleasantly upset at her own husband's foolish decision. They all seemed picture perfect for the Upper West Side of Manhattan.

Reese gave kisses all around before heading back in the direction of his apartment. His stomach was loudly telling him that it was lonely, and in need of some friends to play with. Reese grabbed a smoothie from his local juice shop to curb the rage of hunger.

Walking into his apartment, Reese noticed the flashing light on his answering machine. As he slurped on the juice's large straw, he listened to one of Taylor's typical check-in messages.

"Hey, it's me. Just calling to see how you are doing and was thinking maybe we could just chill tonight. You know, the two of us. My place. I'll make dinner or order in. We'll have some cocktails and a cheesy movie or two. Call me."

Reese immediately felt better. He hadn't had a movie night with Taylor in several months and was glad that she had pried herself away from Heath to make herself available. He wanted to spend time with someone who knew what was going on and would have some truthful, even harsh, advice. After calling Taylor back and confirming their plans, Reese showered and got ready to run several errands during the afternoon. He had to get some groceries, conduct his weekly scouting the new releases at his local book and music store, as well as checkout the end of winter sales at a couple of his favorite stops along Columbus Avenue. Reese had decided that the only way he was not going to sit around his apartment all day moping about Matt's absence was if he sedated himself with the strongest drug he knew: the shopping high.

*   *   *

Exiting the 72nd Street subway station near Taylor's Upper East Side apartment, Reese walked with lightness in his step that had been absent there for a long time. Successfully picking up several sweaters, a couple pairs of distressed jeans and some delightful Chianti before heading to Taylor's place had been a pleasant break from the nearly constant thought he was putting into his relationship with Matt, and now the asshole maneuver pulled by Adam the night before.

After announcing himself to Taylor's doorman, Reese took the express elevator to her forty-fourth floor expanse and let himself in the door she had propped open.

"Beware of fags bearing gifts!" he announced as he saw Taylor covered in her infamous homemade spaghetti sauce. "I see you are cooking without the telephone this evening. Well, I brought reinforcements." He raised the clear bag containing three bottles of wine above his head.

"Christ! This could get messy," she said, pointing to the table with Bombay Sapphire Gin and the two martini glasses on ice.

Noticing the significant spread of food laid out on her kitchen counter, Reese exclaimed, "Hey Martha! I didn't know you were going all out."

"Don't go there, bitch. I paid the nice people at Zabar's to prepare most of this spread. Unlike other self-proclaimed goddesses of the kitchen and home, I didn't force some underpaid migrant worker to make it for me and pan it off as my own."

"Sure. Sure. Just be a good little criminal and tell me before your stock plummets. Anyway, where's my cocktail?" Reese chirped while clapping his hands with excitement. "I've been here more than two minutes and my paws are still without companion."

"You can shake that shaker just as good as I can. I'm making dinner, you can pour the drinks."

Two drinks later and after many curses from Taylor whenever her sauce would explode like a volcano onto her stove, the two friends settled down for dinner and the first of their teen trash movie selections.

"So, how is Matt," she asked sheepishly.

"He's fine, although there was a report on ESPN's talk show *Pardon the Interruption* talking about gay professional athletes. He was listed with all the usual suspects as one who has to struggle with the rumors. There was a mention of the fight we witnessed and that was about it."

"That's still horrible."

"Well, he brought it on himself," Reese said coldly. "While I totally believe that he must come out and get it over with, I'm not willing to make it a priority in the relationship. Although, it's getting harder and harder to ignore."

"Do you think he will ever come out?"

"I don't know," he said sadly. "For his own happiness, I wish he would."

"Don't you mean your own happiness?"

"Wha—"

"You know I love you, Reese," she said after holding in her deep breath to control her look of concern. "But are you trying to get Matt to come out for him or for you?"

"I can't believe you just said that to me," Reese said while pushing his food away from him. "He's lying to everyone about who he is!"

"Yes, he is. But he's doing it because he's in a much higher position than when you came out. He has to do what's best for him, and on his own terms."

Reese was dumbfounded at Taylor's argument. While he had hoped to get a fresh opinion on the issue, he honestly believed that she would have told him to leave Matt before she would endorse Reese assisting in living his lie. "Sometimes you have to know when the fight isn't yours," she said. "All you can do is love and support him."

The two friends continued to eat as Reese tried to digest Taylor's reasoning and keep his dinner from coming back up. Finally looking to lighten the mood, he exclaimed, "Oh my God. I totally forgot to tell you. Guess who I ran into last night when I was out with Benjie?"

"Another run in with Carrot Top?"

"The Bastard."

"No way! What did you do? I hope you threw a drink in his face."

"Actually. We ended up talking a bunch at Hell after Benjie deserted me."

"News flash!"

"Yeah, I know," Reese said, trying not to skip a beat. "And

then we went to a late dinner where he admitted all of the problems in our relationship were because of him. He even said he changed, too!"

"You slept with him!"

"No! Nothing like that," Reese laughed, knowing that it was a pretty fair question even with Matt in the picture. Taylor knew all too well of Reese's unhealthy attraction to his ex-boyfriend. Their relationship had been a mess, and Taylor was there to pick up the pieces time and time again. Of course, she expected to have to do it one more time when she heard his name spoken. "But he couldn't hold it together the entire night. As I finished eating, the cracks showed and it was all a scam. He was playing me 'cause he wanted to know who I wrote my column about."

"Bastard!"

"We've already established that. But the real sad news from the evening was that he looked fabulous. Great haircut, bigger chest and shoulders . . ."

"Oh, let it go!" she exclaimed after she sucked up her last linguine noodle. "Hello, while you might not be having the most fabulous relationship, you are dating a great guy. Why don't you just relax about Matt and see what happens."

"Oh no!" Taylor shrieked as she frantically grabbed the television remote and began flipping before stumbling on to *The O'Reilly Factor*, where her father was that night's featured guest.

"What the hell is wrong with you?" Reese asked before following Taylor's horrified stare to the television. "Oh my God, what is he doing now?"

Taylor and Reese sat in silence as they watched the television with an intensity that they normally reserved for their spending sprees at the Barney's Co-Op Sale. The best friends watched Senator Sheehan earn more and more of Bill O'Reilly's respect by agreeing with the pundit's views on affirmative action, welfare reform and his continued criticism of former President Clinton.

"Does he have nothing better to do than still crack jokes at Clinton's expense? Did he miss the memo that he's not the president anymore?" Taylor inquired, trying her best to reinforce the differences between her father and herself.

"No. I'm sure he's quite aware. Unfortunately, Tay, your daddy and his Republican friends figured out a while ago that the way to stay in power is to focus on scandals that have media staying power. Like it or not, sex in the White House makes good ratings."

"I can't believe anyone still gives a shit about all that. Infidelity has no party loyalty."

"I don't think half the country can stomach most of the Republican platform, let alone try to picture them knocking boots," Reese said, trying to shake the image of Bob and Libby getting it on. "But, the simple fact is they have better sound bites. If the Democrats could just put aside their apparent need for legitimacy, they could easily upstage those assholes."

"I dunno honey. Whenever I go back to Mississippi, I end up shaking in the corner, whimpering 'There's no place like SoHo, There's no place like SoHo.' But there's a reason my dad keeps getting elected and has even been talking with some of his biggest supporters about a run for the White House. The City isn't like the rest of the country, sweetie."

Continuing to drink their wine freely, occasionally looking at each other in astonishment to the responses spewing out of Senator Sheehan's mouth, the duo were treated to an affirmation of Taylor's earlier opinion of the nation during the call-in portion of the program.

"Hi. My name is Nicholas Thompson. I live in Albany, New York. First of all, I just want to thank you Bill for having the best program on television. I get so tired of the the liberal media and their propaganda. You're the only person who just reports the straight-up truth. Maybe we need you in the Oval Office, with respect to the great Senator from Mississippi, of course."

"Thank you Mr. Thompson. That's what the No-Spin Zone on the Factor is all about. Do you have a question for Senator Sheehan?"

"I was just calling to thank him for everything that he stands for. No matter what we do here in my state, we keep sending

Democrats to Washington. So, I'm grateful that he's there to fight the good fight. I wanted to ask the Senator how he plans to fight the proposal by Senator Clinton to allow gay couples to have the same tax benefits as real married couples. Someone has to stop the liberals from advancing the gay agenda before they ruin the whole country, and I figure Senator Sheehan is the one to do the fighting."

As the two friends sat, listening to Senator Sheehan's rant on homosexuals and their staining of the American fabric, Taylor's stomach turned her heavy pasta. She was unnerved by her father's beliefs and was unwilling to look her friend in the eye. After she heard her father say something to the effect of branding the gays with a national registration program, Taylor quickly turned off the television.

When she did manage to face her friend, she found he wasn't angry at all. He was deathly pale.

"Reese, honey, don't let him get to you. He's an ass, and generally, he doesn't really believe in most of the shit he spouts out in interviews. He just knows what he has to say to get elected," she said, reaching out to him, attempting to convince him and herself that she spoke the truth.

"It's not your dad who's the ass, Tay," he said with an unsteady voice. "I'm the ass. I've been fucking up with Matt 'cause I couldn't fathom the fact that people in this country would still hate him, or me, because of who we are. I'd expect it from some guy from your hometown, but that guy was from New York. I mean, granted, upstate is conservative, but people in the northeast aren't suppose to be like that. I've been telling him to do something he knew would be terrible."

*　　*　　*

Later that night, Reese was safely in his bed. Away from Fox News and political pundits and U.S. Senators that had far too much power and far too much reach. His boyfriend was at the other end of the phone, and Reese's tune had drastically changed.

"People are sheep," he said, trying to brush the topic under the rug with O'Reilly's voice still echoing in his head. This was Reese's latest tactic for the issue that occupied his relationship, especially since the Knicks were now in control of the last playoff spot.

He convinced himself that they shouldn't rock the boat by making history. Plus, who was he to really make such a big decision for another person, let alone his boyfriend who was hundreds of miles away on his final road trip of the season.

Matt desperately wanted to argue that it wasn't the sheep, but the wolves that taunted him by calling him "faggot." Like clockwork, the wolves always waited to bark at the quietest moments in his free throw attempts. While Matt had grown to expect them, he also had grown more than tired from them.

"Honey, this isn't the time to think about this," Reese pleaded over the phone, knowing there were only two games left in the season and the Knicks desperately needed to win both of them. "People are going to say what they want, when they want. It goes back to fans being fanatics. Hell, it's the spectacle of the Roman Coliseum with the people wanting to see blood and death. You can't worry about this. It won't do you any good. Just focus on the present. You have a wonderful career opportunity. You're a starter in the National Basketball Association. You can make Knicks history by leading them to the postseason in what seems like their longest playoff drought ever."

"Well, it's kind of difficult to hit my shots when they're calling me 'fudge packer,' or worse."

"I thought it was the hottie in the second row with the tight ass that broke your concentration," Reese quipped.

"Fuck you," Matt chuckled as he smiled for the first time since he left his boyfriend five days earlier. "I love you."

"Aww, that's sweet. Thank you!"

"Smart ass!"

"I love you, too."

Hanging up the phone, Matt wrestled the extra pillow he ordered from housekeeping into place. It mimicked a smaller and softer Reese beside him. He longed to be in a place where his lover could crawl into his nook under his right arm against his chest every night, like the girlfriends, wives and mistresses of his teammates.

"Someday," he wished as he drifted off to sleep.

Chapter Sixteen

Fighting back from eighteen points down in Chicago, Matt led the way in the fourth quarter. His nine points in the last three minutes coming off of two pull-up jumpers, a three pointer and a fast-break dunk, pulled New York within two points.

Now settling in the half court with the final seconds of the game ticking away, Wayne held the ball, calling for Matt to take a three-point jumper off the left baseline. After Wayne pick and rolled with Twan from the top of the key, he met two defenders in the lane where he kicked the ball out to Matt. Standing alone, twenty-four feet from the rim, the former college All-American, and underused professional reserve, caught the ball and stroked it cleanly. The result was nothing but the bottom of the net.

Buzzer.

Knicks win 111-110.

The home crowd was stunned as its beaten Bulls were at the losing end of a last second shot. Those fans were getting to know too well, what the other teams in the League knew when a Michael Jordan-led Chicago routinely feasted on stealing games and sending their fans home dejected.

"ONE GAME!! ONE GAME!!" Coach Baker shouted as he ran onto the court to embrace Matt and Wayne who converged near the free throw line. "One more win and we're in. Focus men!! We can get this done."

Matt stood there for what seemed like an eternity as he watched the mania envelope his teammates. It looked like all was lost as they saw themselves sitting at home during the playoffs once again, but this year they had responded. They fought back and stole a game that shouldn't have been theirs to win. Now the Knicks were heading back to New York to play the dreaded Celtics. If they won this last game, the New York franchise would clinch the final spot in the playoffs.

Back in the locker room Matt was greeted with a text message from Reese. "I knew you could *stroke* it. Talk to you tonight. Love, R"

"Only Boston is left, man," Wayne called out as he made his way to the shower. "Who said they didn't believe?"

The team roared to the satisfaction of nearly everyone.

Matt kept his brief smile before catching the miserable gaze of Anthony's eyes upon him. It was obvious he cared less about the team win and more about his limited play. He had recorded an all-time low eleven minutes before not seeing any action after the beginning of the fourth quarter. Matt was the new star shooting guard, and Anthony's eyes proved it.

As he thought back to the Knicks' improbable run of winning twelve of the last thirteen games, Matt finally began to feel like he was living up to his billing as the basketball star back in college and at White Hall Academy. His unshakable shot and smart play had been a major cause for the streak, but he knew all too well that the rumors swirling around his sexuality were now louder than ever. Matt tried to use them as motivation, but he still prayed that the four signs in the stands that night calling him out as a "butt pirate" and "faggot" would fade away into a sea of cheers for his skill at putting a ball through a hoop.

Coach Baker made his way to the center of the locker room and called for everyone's attention. "Men, I just want to say how proud I am of you. We were down, not only tonight, but this entire season. You all have found a way to win and get the job done. We have one more game to go before we reach our goal. We have to keep the oars on the ship moving, so let's not drop them into the river just yet. The Celtics in two days! At home! In the Garden!"

The room started to cheer as the entire team looked forward to the end of their arduous season, as well as the challenge of making another run at the postseason. The Knicks had played the Celtics three times this season and had been the loser every time. While the coaches and players seemed unsettled with the idea of playing them one last time, especially with so much at stake, they knew that they had revenge and a spot in the playoffs as motivation.

"I know you guys have a few media commitments to do, but let's wrap up all that and get on our flight back to the City," Coach Baker shouted above the fray of men running to and from the shower and getting worked over by the athletic trainers. "And one last thing, no practice tomorrow. I want you fresh for the game on Tuesday. But you guys can come by tomorrow afternoon and we will assist in any shooting drills you guys want to work through to stay sharp."

Coach Baker had become infamous with his players during an earlier losing streak when grueling practices and arduous pre-game meetings dissecting opponent's tendencies had been the norm. When the tide changed and the Knicks began to work together in concert and put a bunch of "W's" on the win column, the coach had backed off. Always a go-with-the-flow type of conductor, Coach Baker didn't want to ruin the goodwill the team was riding to get into this position. But with the importance of Tuesday night's game, he wasn't going to be too cavalier with his team's chance to lockup a spot in the postseason. Everyone knew that the "shooting drills" he would be putting the squad through were anything but optional.

The players and coaches alike finished their post-game routines of getting clean and collecting their assortment of painkillers and bags of ice for their sore joints. Finally, when nearly everyone on the team was aboard the bus to the airport, the New York Knicks moved out, back towards home and hopefully the playoffs.

Anthony had chosen to stay the night with some friends in Chicago and promised the team's management that he'd be in New York the following day. "I don't think Coach Baker gives a damn about him anyway," Wayne confessed as he and Matt talked in the very back of the bus under the radar from the rest of their teammates. "I'm sure they're tryin' to move him. ESPN's Aldridge axed me about it a few days ago after the game with da Bucks. I was tryin' to talk about us an' the playoffs, but he kept askin' about playin' with you."

"God, that would be great," Matt said. If the organization was looking to trade Anthony, they were resolved to hand over the starting job to Matt on a full-time basis. "Of course, they have to decide on whether to re-sign me."

"Casper, what the fuck are you smokin'?"

"Eh?"

"You're golden," he continued. "Baker loves you and he hates the Kid. The Kid fucked his fate in that game early in the season where he refused to shoot 'out of protest.' Like that bitch ever saw a shot he didn't like. All I can do when I play wit' him is bring up the ball and give it to him. I don't think he lets anyone else touch it before he misses whatever shot he thinks he gonna make."

With the chartered flight, the Knicks were back in New York before one in the morning and Matt was back in his own bed shortly after that. Reese had called Matt's cell phone and left a message, saying that he was sorry but he was working on this week's column. Apparently he had already promised it to his editor and couldn't come over until he e-mailed it in. It had been the first time Reese had stood strong to Matt's endless presumptions of his boyfriend's availability.

While Matt wished his boyfriend lay beside him in bed, he liked the idea that Reese wasn't there. It comforted him that Reese had grown comfortable enough in their relationship to tell Matt "no." He hoped that Reese wasn't starting a new trend, but a couple of "no's" here and there would keep things interesting and Matt on his proverbial toes.

After drifting off to sleep, Matt was woken by the fifth ring of his cell phone. Hoping that the caller would just go away, he finally succumbed to it when it rang once again immediately after the first call went to voicemail. It was Ira, his agent.

"Ira, you better have locked up a Nike deal to be the heir to Jordan's shoe line for this," Matt said to his own amusement.

After a long pause in which neither man spoke, Matt heard Ira's cold voice sound through his tiny cell phone. "It broke."

Ira's heart-stopping coldness continued as he explained that the *New York Post* gave Knicks' beat writer Kevin Ashbie the front page for a story citing a source within the New York franchise, confirming Matt as a homosexual. The first print edition had already hit the street, and it was already on the *Post's* website. Ira also said the Associated Press was about to release their version citing Ashbie's story.

According to Ashbie's story, the inside source said that they witnessed Matt kiss men and take them back to his hotel room on the road. The source also said that "loud sex-like noises" came from the room nearly every night when the team was on the road and away from New York.

"Goddamn," Matt said as the game versus the Celtics crept into his head. "What the hell? Couldn't this have waited until after Tuesday's game?"

"Well, it's here and we have to do something," Ira said. "I have already been called to comment. I thought about an injunction, but what judge will grant that at two in the morning? Look, Matt, I'm going to be on the first plane in the morning. Do not talk to anyone. I'm sure it is only a matter of time until they locate your cell and home phone numbers. We will make a statement once I get up there."

Tossing the phone across the room, Matt finally understood what was driving Reese during his tirades against cell phones. Reese had always thought phones should be able to be hung up in anger. Hitting the little red "end" button wasn't exactly befitting the moment. He laughed as he reached for his home phone to call his boyfriend.

*   *   *

"Hello?" Reese said with sleep obviously in his voice.

"Baby, I'm sorry to wake you," Matt said in a calm, even tone. "But, it's happened."

As Reese tried to knock the fatigue from his head, Matt recounted his conversation with Ira. Reese was unable to speak, let alone think of anything useful to say. Finally Reese looked out his window and noticed the papers being delivered to the all-night deli across from his apartment. He mumbled, "Let me call you back. I'm heading out to grab a copy of the paper. I'll talk to you in five."

Getting dressed as quickly as he could, Reese dashed out into the night, seeking the latest the papers had to offer. The street was freezing from a pouring spring rain and his feet were growing desperately cold from the water seeping into his old running shoes.

"Socks would have been useful," he said as he walked past two drunks and a drug dealer outside Saint Clare's Hospital. Entering the deli, Reese saw the stack of newly arrived *New York Posts* with an action shot of Matt playing defense in the game versus Chicago. Matt was bent over in what Reese assumed was the proper defensive stance to challenge his opponent, but the image, with its headline screaming, "MATTY LIKES BOYS!" was a desperate attempt to appear as homoerotic as possible. The headline continued, "Inside Source tells of rampant sex parties and hidden life of Knick glory boy," while another line resting underneath in a much smaller font continued, "Knicks win, 111-110, One Game From Playoffs."

The night clerk didn't look up from reading his own copy of the story as Reese dropped his quarter on the counter and began reading Kevin Ashbie's exclusive. With his trained journalistic eye highly scrutinizing every line, Reese saw that Kevin had done his job by sticking to the facts and not making any unwarranted claims that the brash headline had alluded to. Of course, the damage was still incomprehensible as Reese continued reading.

There were no dates or names to back up the source's accusations, which Kevin was diligent to state over and over again.

There were only grand elusive statements, which read like a decree. "Matty likes the boys. He brings them on the road and ain't shy about kissing and hugging them in front of everybody. Coach don't want to talk about it, and nobody else wants to talk about it either." Kevin noted that the team had been one of the hottest in the League and was on the verge of making the playoffs for the first time in many seasons.

Reese had no clue which of the New York Knicks had been this story's Deep Throat, and it seemed completely irrelevant at this point. When he asked his boyfriend later on the phone as they scrutinized the story together, Matt said the suspects were limited. But he conceded with nearly thirty people traveling around with the team on most occasions, it would be very difficult to say which one blew the whistle or cared enough to take it public in the first place.

"The obvious answer is Anthony, because he and I don't get along. Plus he has the most to gain if we fail since he isn't a part of the wins," Matt argued. "But it could be anyone since these allegations are all bullshit. I've never done anything in front of anyone. And what is that shit about me taking boys back to my room every night? Damn, I wish I had that much sex!"

Reese believed Matt and knew how people who became inside sources tended to exaggerate to "sell" their story. But thankfully, there was no mention of Reese. It would have been a major piece of reporting if he had been named as Matt's lover. The two men hadn't been seen together publicly since the restaurant after Heath's brawl.

Reese had even turned down invitations to more parties at Matt's gallery. At the time, Reese said no because he didn't want to be forced into dealing with Matt on a public stage where they could show no sign that the two had been doing the funky butt love, let alone acknowledge the other's presence in more than a polite approach. But, Reese's reservation now proved to have helped keep his name out of the story.

As Reese argued this point, he found his answering machine blinking. "Did you leave a message while I was out getting the paper?" he asked while pressing play. After hearing a negative response, Reese conceded that he hadn't checked his machine since he went over to Taylor's place to watch the game earlier that night. It had been two-consecutive nights on the Upper East Side, which was two too many for Reese if he wanted to keep his sanity.

After another dozen hang-ups, Reese finally heard, "Reese, this is Kevin Ashbie from the *New York Post*. We met a couple of months back in Philadelphia. I've been trying to reach you for a couple of days now, but haven't left a message. If you could give me a call back when you get this, I would appreciate it. I'm on deadline."

The tag from Kevin's message said it was left an hour after the end of the Knicks' victory over Chicago. Reese's heart began to race and a desperate feeling of fear rushed through his body. Kevin didn't know for sure that Reese was Matt's lover, but apparently he knew enough to suspect it. Reese thought if Kevin were at all the decent reporter he suspected he was, Kevin would inevitably link Reese's sudden attendance at Knicks games to Matt's now headlining sexuality.

"Was that Kevin on your machine?" Matt asked.

Reese finally became disgusted with his own disbelief that he wasn't just Matt's friend who was attending a few NBA games. While he appreciated Matt's risk in having his boyfriend there, Reese now read the headline again and truly understood the risk that Matt had taken. Reese chided his own arrogance and the way that he nearly flaunted his presence in the stands. He wasn't just a friend of the starting shooting guard. Reese was, on the simplest level, the fag columnist for *The Village Voice*.

Chapter Seventeen

"The trucks are backed up all the way to Prince Street!" Heath shouted as he looked down from their SoHo loft. "Damn boy, I didn't know you suckin' cock would get all these news guys, CNN and Hardcopy, too! Do we have a camera? I want to get a picture of this."

Taylor jabbed Heath in his side, hoping to curb her boyfriend's enthusiasm and asked, "Matt, what does your agent say?"

"I should head out and give them my stock picks for the next six months. That would give my portfolio at least a fifteen, maybe twenty, percent boost," Heath said as he continued to marvel at the media compound that was growing on Dominick Street.

At his latest count he found no less than eight camera crews from various networks and news organizations lurking around his building's front door. Heath was positive there were a slew of print and Internet reporters down there as well, but without their large cameras and spotlights piercing through the early morning sky cluttered by mist and dense fog, he couldn't spot them as easily.

Ignoring his roommate, Matt answered, "Ira says I should make a statement. He's on a flight now up from Washington and should be here within the hour."

Matt sank back into his leather couch with his hands rubbing his eyes as if he could wipe them clean of all the problems he saw facing him. "What am I going to do?" he asked to anyone with an answer that would come from neither Heath nor Taylor.

Matt had held himself together for the most part since Ira called him nearly four hours earlier, but with Manhattan and the rest of his world set to wake up and not only read the breaking news from the *Post*, but see it on any channel with a news room, Matt was quickly losing his cool.

"You knew this day was going to happen at some point," Heath said coldly. "I wish it wasn't two days before the biggest game of the year, but these are the cards that you've been dealt."

"Reese is on his way over," Taylor said as she read the text message from her phone. "He says that he has to see you."

"He can't come here!" Matt screamed. "The media is all over the place."

"He said he was going to dress up," Taylor explained. "He was a delivery boy for Halloween last year. One of his less creative ideas, for sure."

"Call him and tell him not to come," Matt shouted. "I haven't figured out what I'm going to do, and until that happens, I don't want the media reporting that I'm hanging out with my boyfriend."

Taylor silently dialed her best friend's number when a buzzer at the door went off. While Heath looked through the peephole to see who it was, an eerie silence fell upon the loft. Two photographers and a camera crew had worked their way up into the building earlier that morning when Heath had made his way outside for cups of coffee and doughnuts from Krispy Kreme. Unfortunately for the reporters, who expected anything but a scantily clad woman greeting them, they found Taylor covered only in one of Heath's dress shirts when she opened the door. Expecting to find her boyfriend, she was taken aback when an obese cameraman and a pair of photographers managed to snap a few shots of her slight frame.

"It's Ira," Heath said as he unhitched the three locks on the loft's front door.

Three gentlemen, all of whom were much younger and larger than the nerdy agent, escorted Ira. Two of them looked like former offensive lineman fresh from a career in the NFL and wore dark sunglasses and earpieces.

The last one to enter the apartment was Ira's shadow. Terry was a sniveling man who had the honor of carrying Ira's briefcase and cell phone. Matt couldn't think of a worse existence, until he saw Terry's eyes full of pity for the entangled NBA star.

"Matt, how are you holding up?" Ira asked, moving past Heath and Taylor to his overwhelmed client. "I'm sure this is a big inconvenience for you, with the final regular season game tomorrow night just forty blocks away."

"You could say that again," Heath said as Matt was choosing to or just not willing to talk. "So Ira what's the plan? Payoffs? Murder? Or good old-fashioned blackmail? We all know that you have the goods on everyone. So what'll it be?"

"Why don't you go out and start choking them all?" Ira replied coldly before continuing, "I hear you're pretty good at doing that."

Taylor let out a snort of a laugh and introduced herself.

"Yes, yes," Ira said courtly. "I met you before at one of your father's functions. I'm sure he will be not too pleased to hear that you're mixed up in this mess."

"Mess?" Matt whimpered from his still sunken position along the couch. "I wish it was only a mess."

"Yes, it's a mess," Ira said coldly. "But you are right, Matt. This is a mess of the greatest proportion. We have worked for three years to be in this position. You are a starter leading your franchise into the playoffs and up for a contract extension and that can all be lost if we don't handle this properly. But now there is this story . . . you and some other boy."

"Ira, I'm not a boy!" Matt yelled.

"I didn't think so, but your actions have been just as irresponsible as a child's. So you do the math."

"I don't think his actions brought this about," Heath argued. "Matt has been more than reserved in his approach to dating."

"Yes, and you are the one to judge this. You being so reserved yourself," Ira quipped. "But don't worry Matt, I am here to clean it up, again."

Heath, Taylor and Matt all sat back as Ira outlined his plan of action. First there was to be a statement of denial with a released picture of Matt and Alex establishing that the two are a happy couple. Secondly, Ira said there would be no press conference, insisting that Matt was concentrating on working with his team to ensure a win against Boston and a spot in the playoffs for the Knicks. "But to keep you further from the public's eye, you will stay at the Trump International Hotel for the next few days with these two boys as your security detail. It would be great if we could get Alex and you out on the town for dinner or something to that effect. Maybe dinner at Jean Georges at the hotel. They can handle it. Their staff is discreet beyond measure but could accommodate us for this photo op."

"I don't understand why Matt doesn't come clean now," Taylor asked with her voice quivering in fear of the wrath she expected from Ira.

"Because, he must make the playoffs. It is worth millions to Matt, as well as to the owners who pay his salary," Ira reasoned. "If he were to tell the truth now, it would be even more of a distraction and any attempt at the postseason would be a token one at that. No, the thing to do is protect everyone's interest and deny everything."

"Ira's right," Matt said as he lifted himself off the couch. "I'll pack a bag and be ready to leave in ten minutes."

"Excellent. I will head down and issue the statement on your behalf," Ira said as he and his entourage quickly exited the loft and proceeded into the mob of media waiting below.

Heath watched as all the cameras and reporters lined up to get position on Ira and his minions who formed a near perfect black backdrop for the cameras behind the agent. "What a piece of work he is," he said in amazement. "But you gotta hand it to him, he's pretty damn good."

"What are you talking about," Taylor said in bewilderment. "How can denying who Matt is be a good thing?"

"It's a business, Taylor," Heath said as he rolled his eyes at his girlfriend's naivety. "I doubt that Ira would endorse a plan to keep Matt in the closet for much longer. This lie, or misdirection, will only serve as a Band-Aid until the issue can be dealt with in a more comfortable environment. Ira's too good at what he does to do something of this magnitude when it could irreparably harm Matt's chances to stay in the League."

*   *   *

Matt was waiting for his boyfriend to appear in the rented penthouse on the 44th floor where Central Park West meets Columbus Circle, and the rich and fabulous escape Manhattan, if only to seek refuge high in a tower above it. The New York Knick had barely escaped his own downtown prison with his agent in tow earlier when their hired guns paved a six-foot path from the front of his apartment building to a waiting car parked out front. The unrelenting cameramen and loudmouthed reporters, who were trying to outscoop their peers who stood side by their side, made the three-step walk nearly impossible.

But Matt's loft had become impractical to stay at, as his cell phone and home number had been leaked to the press, and the incoming calls were as continuous as the onslaught of photographers banging on the apartment's front door. The cameramen had even resorted to climbing into positions outside the loft's floor-to-ceiling windows. Finally after Heath called in the police, the paparazzi retreated into the building across the street. The cameras were now recording all the movement within the loft from squatting at some of Matt's slimiest neighbors who cashed in their living room space for a few hundred dollars.

Now safely in the exclusive Upper West Side hotel, Matt was safe from the latest offensives from the New York press corp. Ira had secured the two hired security guards standing ominously at Matt's penthouse door, while Donald Trump's own private army guarded the rest of the property. Trump's team had a first class reputation for working diligently with superstars and others with skyscraping profiles to ensure only the most exclusive members of society made their way onto his properties.

It had been over an hour since Matt called Reese and told him where he was staying. With Trump International being only blocks from Reese's own Hell's Kitchen apartment, Matt thought his lover should have arrived more than a half-hour ago. After getting off the phone with his boyfriend, Matt had ordered up a buffet of lunch options for them to feast on while they digested the last twelve hours. That had arrived and now cooled past its edibility. Something was up, and Matt was tired of it.

"Where are you?" Matt hissed into his cell phone when he heard his boyfriend answer it on its third ring.

"I guess I'm right outside your door," Reese said. Matt heard in his boyfriend's tone that he was annoyed as Matt was from the delay. "I would have been inside a while ago, but your goons are holding me hostage."

"What? I told them that you were coming." Matt said as he ran downstairs to the duplex's front doors. "What the fuck is wrong now?"

"I'm sorry, sir," answered the taller of the two security guards. "But we are under strict orders from Mr. Pilton to only allow anyone to see you if he agrees to them. We've been waiting for him to give us a decision on Mr. Gibbons, but he hasn't answered."

"Is he on the phone now?" Matt demanded while pointing to the other guard that was glued to his cell phone. "Give me the phone."

"Ira, what the fuck?" Matt continued while raising his voice into the security guard's cell phone. "You can't hold me a prisoner here. If I want someone to come over, then they're coming over."

"Matt, please lower you voice," Ira said coolly. "I just wanted to ensure that no one snuck by and caused a bigger problem. But, hearing that you invited this man over, I was stunned to say the least. Do you know about him? Did you know that he's a gay columnist for *The Village Voice*?"

"Jesus Christ!" Matt shrieked. "He's my boyfriend, Ira. I think I know what he does for a living."

"Will you please lower your voice," Ira continued from the other end of the phone. "You never know who will hear you."

"I thought this was a safe place, Ira," Matt said, patronizing his agent. "Didn't you say that I would be safe here? Didn't you say they are 'discreet beyond measure'?"

"Matt, don't act like a child. This is why I told the security detail to clear all visitors with me. You don't know what's good for you, let alone helpful in remedying this situation. Now for the sake of clearing this mess up, can you start referring to Mr. Gibbons as a friend, or better yet, an acquaintance?"

"I am not going to call Reese my acquaintance!" Matt yelled into the phone. "Would you call your wife that?"

"If it would help me in securing a contract in the neighborhood of fifty to seventy million dollars, I would, yes. And frankly, you need to see the writing on the wall, Matt. You and I both know that you could score thirty points tomorrow night and thirty in every game en route to the Knicks' first championship in thirty years, and I still couldn't get you signed to a minimum deal with any other club in the League—let alone any endorsements—if you don't play ball. This has become a bigger mess and is exploding in the media. We might have to make another statement, and establish a better cover than that damn J. Crew model."

"Shut the fuck up, Ira." Matt yelled. "When I score thirty-five tonight and get the Knicks into the postseason for the next five years, I won't have you as an agent. So don't you fucking worry about it. You're fired." Matt threw the phone to the second security guard and said, "I would appreciate if you two would stay here. I just fired Ira, but I will cover your costs."

After the two men agreed, Matt took his speechless boyfriend into the penthouse, and let out a howl of laughter. "Are you all right?" Reese asked. "You look like you're about to lose it."

"I've already lost it, baby," he said while sitting down on a white leather couch that had probably seen more famous bottoms than the top studio executives in Hollywood. "Damnit, that felt good. I never liked that man, but now I have no one to run interference for me." Matt turned pale as he continued, "I don't know what I'm going to do, Reese."

"Well, whatever you do, you might want to talk to the press. I was watching CNN and ESPN this morning and all they were talking about was your non-statement, statement."

"Ira said something else should be said," Matt said with a

heavy heart. "But that was before I fired him. I don't even know what he released to the press this morning."

"It was something to the effect that you are too busy to deal with silly accusations when you're this close to the playoffs," Reese paraphrased.

"I don't want to do a press conference. I have a shoot around with the team at three in the Garden."

"So, don't have a press conference," Reese argued. "Why don't you just pick up the phone and call one guy and let him have an exclusive. You could talk slower and tell your story easier. I'm sure you could have a reporter up here in twenty minutes, if you wanted to."

"I'll call the Knicks press office and have them arrange something small," Matt concluded before leaning in and receiving his first kiss from his lover in more than four days. "But, what am I going to say?"

*   *   *

Settling into one of the media workrooms along the luxury suites at Madison Square Garden, Matt sat down with Leonard Murphey, a respected journalist for the *New York Times*. While Leonard hadn't written a word on the topic of Matt's sexuality, the Knicks shooting guard thought that if Leonard would write something conclusive on the matter, the whole story would go away.

The award-winning journalist didn't hesitate when he received Matt's noon phone call with an offer for an exclusive interview. "I've always been a fan of your writing," Matt said on the phone. "This matter has just been a great burden on my shoulders and I would like to set the record straight."

Leonard was a little man, no more than five and a half feet tall. He was balding and the hair he did have had turned prematurely gray, making him look much older than he was. The journalist carried a folder, which had been packed with clippings. Matt believed that with only a few hours to prepare, the entire research department at the *Times* had dedicated themselves to getting Leonard up to speed on the issue.

"Do you have a prepared statement that you would like to start with?" he asked while flipping his tape recorder to the on position. "Perhaps something about you firing your agent this morning."

Damn, these guys were good, Matt thought to himself. "I didn't realize that you guys would already know about it."

"Mr. Pilton released a statement a few hours ago."

"Oh," Matt said not knowing what to say. "I don't think it would be proper to discuss that."

"Well, I'm not here to report on your business dealings. So, Matt, no statement?"

Matt shook his head from side-to-side and wanted to kill himself for not thinking about what he was going to say. He figured he would just deny, deny, deny, like he had done all of his life. There was no real reason to change that time-tested and proven tactic.

"Matt, care to respond to the allegation by Henry Fulton?"

"I'm sorry, what?"

"Mr. Fulton held a press conference an hour ago and said that he was a former boyfriend of yours."

Matt was stunned that one of his former boyfriends would come out of the cracks to stoke the fire. Of course, things didn't end on the happiest note with Henry, but Matt never would have expected this type of play from him.

When there was no answer, the reporter continued, "He said you two were lovers for more than six months and the pressure of the relationship eventually led him to seek psychiatric help after the breakup."

"I don't know who you are talking about," Matt said sheepishly. "I've never heard of Henry Fulton."

"He also released a picture of the two of you in bed together," Leonard said while watching the life drain away from Matt's face. Leonard didn't like what he was about to do, but he thought he had been invited to this train wreck, so he might as well be the one to tell of its disaster. "It was a still frame from a video recording. He claims that he recorded a sexual encounter of the two of you.

"I don't believe . . . ," Matt tried to say, looking around the room for a quick way out.

"It's a very clear shot," Leonard said, throwing the snapshot onto the table. "I'm sure it's possible that it's a forgery. But, let's be honest, Matt. We both know that's you. Tell me what this is about."

Matt continued to search the room for answers. He wished that he hadn't fired Ira so hastily. Ira would have been there for this interview. Ira would have known about Henry's press conference. Ira would have warned him about the photo. Ira would have picked a less-credible reporter!

"Um, I . . . don't know where that came from," he finally said, hoping that something drastic would happen that would cut short the interview. A power outage. An earthquake. He needed a miracle.

"Matt, I just told you where this photo came from," the reporter countered. Watching Matt twitch and squirm in his seat, Leonard finally continued, "This story isn't going to go away. Tell me what's going on and we can set the record straight. Just like you said you wanted to do."

Taking a large gulp of water, Matt tried to compose his thoughts. He wanted this to be over. He didn't like being in this position and he never wanted to be in it again.

"Henry and I were lovers," he said abruptly, but still slinking back into his chair as if he had just been relieved of a great weight upon his shoulders and could now, finally, relax. "But I'm not involved in that anymore."

"Yes, I know," Leonard interjected as his eyes widened and glistened with the possibility of writing the biggest story of the year. "Mr. Fulton said that the relationship was over more than a year ago. He said, off the record, you are seeing someone else now that he knew indirectly."

Matt's mind was racing as he thought of a connection between Reese and Henry. He couldn't think of any, so there must be a reason why Henry only said it off the record. Henry just loved attention and probably went overboard. Then when he was asked about Matt's current situation, Henry answered, "off the record." Matt was sure that was what happened, or at least sure enough. It was all too hard to figure out on the fly, while a reporter sat across from him, looking for answers from his face as well as his voice.

"I'm not seeing anyone right now," Matt said. "In fact, I'm in therapy. I've seen the errors of my ways and am working with the Lord to correct my past. Homosexuality is a sin and I had been tricked by the devil into its filth."

Leonard sat speechless. He couldn't believe what he heard. Not only was he getting the exclusive on the first male athlete in one of the major sports in America to come out while he was still on the roster, but Leonard now had this same athlete damning homosexuality. "Let me get this straight. So you're telling me that you were once a homosexual and now you're reformed. Is that correct?"

Matt took more than a second or two as he felt Leonard's piercing eyes move across his face. He couldn't take the scrutiny of the situation any longer. Matt wanted this to go away. Finally, he muttered, "Yes, that is correct."

There were numerous follow-up questions as Leonard wrote down notes, stopping and starting his tape recorder to allow himself to compose his own thoughts before moving on. Leonard was most inquisitive about Matt's therapy. But, Matt said he wouldn't give out that information to "secure the safety of the God-fearing men who worked to save me."

Matt didn't know how long the interview was going to last. He had talked in circles for what felt like hours. There was no reason to what he was saying except that he believed it would make the whole issue just go away. He had to admit to the past, but convince Leonard that he was moving away from the lifestyle.

Finally, a public relations officer knocked on the door to the room and said that the team's practice was starting in less than fifteen minutes.

"Just one last question, if you don't mind," Leonard pleaded. "Do you know the passage in the Bible that says homosexuality is wrong?"

The Knicks press officer's jaw dropped as he heard Matt say, "Romans 1:26-27."

Chapter Eighteen

Throughout Coach Baker's "optional" shoot around, Matt worked with rest of the ball-handling guards on one-on-one drills, trying to beat their man off the dribble and pull up for a twelve-to-fifteen-foot jump shot on the wings off of the lane. The coaching staff had outlined a plan where the guards would direct the Knicks offense directly at Celtics' guard Paul Pierce in hopes of getting him into foul trouble. If Pierce were to become a bench warmer with the threat of fouling out late in the game, the Knicks believed they could steal the game and prevent a season sweep by Boston.

But early on during practice, Matt had been pulling up prematurely from his drives to the basket and leaning too far forward in his shot, resulting in his attempts hitting the back of the iron. He replayed his interview with Leonard Murphey in his head over and over again, with the conclusion that the admission of his past sexual relations with men was enough. To Matt, he thought that was the story and it should be dealt with like any other athlete with a past full of indiscretions. Hell, no one would really be that surprised. He just gave them confirmation. One more day in the press and it would be gone.

"OK, men," Coach Baker shouted after blowing his whistle a little louder than usual. "We looked sharp out there, after settling down. Let's remember the keys to our game. Ball movement through Wayne. Getting the ball into Twan, when he's in position. And, finally, hitting Matt when he's open. Patience on offense and diligence on defense."

Clapping his hands together, Coach Baker sent his squad to

run the stairs of the arena to illustrate that the team still had a long way to go to reach the top, and by only going one step at a time would they reach their goal. But when Matt was about to break into a jog towards section 123, his favorite aisle, the coach called him over for a few words.

"Nice story, huh," he said, watching Matt roll his eyes, petitioning the man for some relief from the cover story of the *New York Post*. "Look, I could care less what you do off the court, as long as it doesn't affect what happens on the court. I, no we, need you to stay focused on the job that is at hand, Matt. We need you tomorrow night, and despite what some asshole said in leaking that story, I'm very proud of you for always thinking of this team first."

Matt listened as his coach went on to say that neither he nor a member of his coaching staff was the one cited in the story. The blistery coach paused as he saw one of the Knicks public relations officials come running up to the two men standing near center court.

"Excuse me, Coach Baker," the nerdy Knick official said, looking more flustered than usual. "But we have a situation with Matt."

"We already know that," the old coach barked at the young man. "It's all anyone can talk about, but what we have to do is keep Matt level and on-routine until and after tomorrow night."

"No, there's more."

The young official explained that there was an unusual amount of media trying to get into practice. "Even with this morning's headline and statement, the number of reporters seem to be growing. And we have protestors."

"Protestors?" Matt asked.

"Yes, from the gay community."

"Why would they be protesting?" the coach asked.

"The *Times* reported from your interview with Leonard that you believe homosexuals are evil, and that they're going to hell."

Matt turned stark white as his coach and the public relations official looked to him for answers. Again, he didn't have any to give. Honestly, he thought that Leonard wouldn't have noted his religious comments. Many celebrities had said more stupid things in their time with reporters than he had done earlier that day.

But now there was a representative from his employer telling him that his foolish comments had been taken seriously. He hadn't just lied to some nobody from the stands who had called him a butt pirate or fudge packer. He had lied to a reporter with one of the world's most powerful news organizations. How could he have been so stupid?

"Matt, forget the stairs," Coach Baker said, breaking the silence. "You better call your agent."

"He fired his agent," the public relations official quickly interjected.

Noticing that there was a growing party at the center of his home court, Wayne walked over to see what was happening with his friend. From the moment he read the headline that morning, he knew Matt was going to be in the middle of a firestorm.

Wayne had known his secret since the NBA All-Star weekend in Matt's rookie season when they laid the foundation for their eventual friendship. Matt was traveling with Wayne because he was scheduled to play in the Rookie Game, while Wayne was to make his third appearance in weekend's main event. But after being grounded by extreme weather in Milwaukee for the first night, Wayne flat out asked his teammate if he liked girls or boys. Citing his own brother's sexual proclivity, Wayne possessed a highly refined gaydar, for a straight man, and told his new friend that it was no big deal. Eventually, Matt broke under the pressure and told his point guard that he was gay.

But now, his friend was in more trouble. Listening to the Knicks media official whom Wayne had talked to millions of times, but still didn't know his name, he found out that Matt was now being a lightning rod for all gay bashers and homophobic zealots that permeated the country. Little did the protestors know, they were calling out one of their own. One who wanted to find his way out of the tunnel, but who, without his friends' help, couldn't even find the light to show him the way.

Shaking his head and looking for Matt's eyes, which seemed to be locked into the center portion of the Knicks logo at the court's middle circle, Wayne tried to think of what his friend could have said to have turned his situation from a nuisance into a full-blown epidemic with major societal repercussions.

"You're fuckin stupid," Wayne told his friend as the two finally left the court. "What did you say to that bitch?"

Matt recalled the interview. It amazed him how it had seemed so harmless just ten minutes ago, but now he could think of each and every misstep he took along that conversation's path. "I just wanted it to go away," he mumbled as the two entered the locker room.

There was an announcement that some reporters were going to be let in for some quick interviews. The players were instructed to talk about the game they had with the Celtics and try to avoid Matt as a topic. Matt was to be ushered away before the media would enter the locker room.

"You know, I knew you were gay before you told me in that airport," Wayne said lightheartedly before turning to look at Matt preparing to run from the locker room and avoid the onslaught of the press. "I didn't think it was that big of a deal. I never thought you were hidin' it, I just thought you ain't advertisin' it. But now, I think I was wrong. You were hidin'. That ain't right. You're a good baller, Matt. You don't need to be ashamed of anything. But, you should be ashamed of this."

*   *   *

His escape from Madison Square Garden was brutal. Matt was lead into the catacombs of the building into the bustling Penn Station that stirred below the most famous arena in the world. After being recognized by two people that were obviously upset with Matt's published remarks from the way they shouted and taunted him, he was escorted with a full security detail, including his own two hired guns, onto the streets of New York and eventually to the corner of Seventh Avenue and 33rd Street where a car was waiting.

Once back in the comforts of his suite at the Trump International Hotel, Matt reached out to his friends who all seemed too busy to talk to him. According to his assistant, Heath was in a meeting with a client. Reese was also not available since he answered neither his cell nor his home phone. Matt thought he would just have to suffer in his own silence, since now he didn't have Ira to fix everything for him.

Turning on the large screen television, Matt settled into the deep couch and flipped the channel to ESPN News. There were numerous reports covering Matt. There was the *New York Post* cover story, Ira's public statement, Ira's firing and now Matt's bizarre statements to the *New York Times*. The past twenty-four hours swirled in his head while he began to meander about the channels, hoping for anything that would serve as a musical interlude to the next segment of his life. Finally, Matt found an all-day marathon of *Trading Spaces* on The Learning Channel and fell asleep as one of the trashy designers draped yet another master bedroom in fabric after removing the homeowner's Don't Touch sign from the room's treasured ceiling fan.

Waking up hours later in his darkened tomb with only the glow from Bob Vila's Home Again peppering the room with light, Matt crawled for his cell phone. It was nearly nine o'clock, and he had still not heard back from Heath, let alone his boyfriend. He decided to see what was going on with Heath. He hadn't heard his roommate's voice since he left his apartment earlier that day under the protection of Ira and the two armed security guards still standing guard outside his suite. Matt was feeling an overwhelming sense of shame for the actions that he took, but certainly Heath would understand. He always did.

"Hey man," Matt said into his cell phone, hoping that Heath wouldn't be too occupied with Taylor to entertain him. "What's going on?"

"I'm pickin' egg shells out of my hair."

"What?"

"I got out of the elevator here at home and turned the corner to the front door," Heath explained. "Waiting for me was a band of militant Chelsea boys, in what I hope was their gayest gear. 'Cause, man, if those weren't their gayest clothes, I feel real bad for the people who claim them in their lives. Damn, it was fuckin' gay. They had cut-off jeans that rode lower on the hip than any of Taylor or Alex's clothes. And, those boys had to shave or something, 'cause the shorts ended just below their package. I think they also had bright pink T-shirts with no arms. I mean it was forty degrees today. What's with gay men and their sleeveless T's?"

"Do you have a point?" Matt asked while he secretly admired Heath for being able to let his mind ramble on and on away from the problems that plagued him.

"Yeah, I have a point," Heath said louder than before. "As soon as I go to unlock our door, they start pelting me with eggs. I think they had hoped they were rotten, but they weren't."

"Well that's good . . ."

"No, it's not Matt. Do you know how hard it is to get egg out of my curly hair? I've washed it three times and spent more than an hour picking through my scalp, looking for pieces of shell. At last count, I think I got hit by eighteen eggs. There is a huge red mark on my left cheek where one barely missed my eye. That's going to look good in the morning meetings with the guys from London, as is the door which they continued to throw shit against while chanting some song. I had security remove them, but I didn't press charges as long as they wouldn't return."

"Why not?"

"Why not?" Heath yelled. "Damnit, Matt. You must be the stupidest son of a bitch, gay or straight. You're a fucking John Rocker now. What they fuck were you thinking?"

"I don't . . ."

"Well, you gotta do something because I wouldn't want to take the floor at the Garden on national television without saying or correcting some of the shit you've been spewing lately."

"It was only today . . ."

"No it isn't, Matt," Heath raged. "It's been your entire fucking life. Stop lying to people. Give them the chance to know you. God knows, the truth can't be worse than it is right now."

"Fuck you. That's easy for you to say. You have nothing to lose."

"Take a look around, Matt. Neither do you." Heath shouted before apparently ending the phone call. Matt sat there stunned from Heath's confrontation. His friend had never pushed Matt to do anything unpleasant or anything that disrupted the flow of their lavish existence. The two men were living a dream in which they were wealthy, attractive and desirable to nearly everyone. Heath had always joked that they had lived in a bubble that shielded them from the real world. It was apparent to everyone, including Matt, that the bubble had finally burst open, laying waist to everyone who was nearby.

Matt cycled through his cell's phonebook and dialed Reese. He knew Reese would be hurt by the comments made to Leonard, but after some smoothing over, he would come around. After the fifth ring on his second consecutive call to Reese's home number, Matt hung up. He had now run through his list of two people that he could trust in a time of crisis and neither one of them wanted to talk to him.

As he flipped through the channels he found the NHL Playoffs where the Washington Capitals were about to be eliminated by the Pittsburgh Penguins yet again. The action in the game was slow and methodical, and Matt yearned for some type of breakaway goal or at the very least a bench-clearing brawl between the two teams.

Matt's stomach turned from the lack of dinner, absent a pear that had been left in the refrigerator from the suite's previous resident, and just when he was about to crack open his third beer of the evening, his guards informed him that he had a visitor.

For a moment his heart fluttered at the idea of Reese walking through the door. But it wasn't his boyfriend who slipped past Tweedle Dee and Tweedle Dum with a carryout bag, and as the first guard went to grab Heath, Matt called off his dogs. "It's all right. Thanks."

"So I thought I better tell you that the gossip pages are naming Reese as your lover tomorrow," Heath said, sporting the earlier reported red blemish upon his cheek. Lifting the bag, which smelled like roasted chicken, and scanning the suite with his eyes, he continued, "I brought some dinner from Carnegie Deli. Eat like men. Be stuffed like pigs. Sleep like babies. Where do you want to chow?"

Matt laughed as he felt his crumbling world start to build up from underneath him once again. He pointed to the couch and said, "I'm the lead on SportsCenter. Apparently, I'm all they can talk about. I've been watching the promos for it throughout the hockey game. It's about to come on. How is the egg shell retrieval coming?"

"I'm sure there are still a few left in there."

"So the bastards finally got to Reese, which I guess I should care about," Matt said, trying to cover his pain from being ignored by his boyfriend. "When he finally decides to talk to me, I'm sure he will call me a hypocrite and ask himself how he could have ever dated someone like me. But that's something I can't control anymore, since he refuses to answer his phone. Three more messages left at home and another four on his cell. All of them not returned."

"It's not easy for him either," Heath said after taking a big bite of his Turkey Rueben without sauerkraut and extra Thousand Island dressing. "Taylor told me that he's been a mess all day. He had the locks changed, so you couldn't break in . . ."

"As if I walk the streets of the City to go knocking on his door."

"But in true Reese fashion, he messengered the new keys to his neighbor at work whom he is key buddies with. After a few hours, Taylor tracked the neighbor down and used that new key to get in when Reese refused to unlock the door for her."

"He's a little crazy," Matt said with a smile that he had hoped went unnoticed. After all, he was now trying to distance himself from his boyfriend.

"Yeah, but you love him."

Chapter Nineteen

With Madison Square Garden in its final preparations for the biggest Knicks game in recent history, the team brass decided to hold Matt's press conference across Seventh Avenue from the arena at the Hotel Pennsylvania. Security was tight, and no one without a written invitation from the League's office would be admitted to the sprawling ballroom that would serve as the media center for the impromptu announcement.

An elevated stage had been constructed in the back corner with a table and chairs for five people. While Matt was the main attraction, the League office wasn't going to lose this opportunity to do some positive public relations with the gay community, if not the American family as a whole. To be seated with the now high-profile athlete was NBA Commissioner David Stern, New York Knick General Manager Aram Mestjian, Knick Coach Dale Baker, as well as Matt's newly rehired agent Ira Pilton.

At Heath's urging, Matt called Ira that morning, apologizing for firing him and requesting him to resume the responsibility of representing and counseling him in the coming months, if not only for the coming hours. "Hell, that bitch knows everyone. If you make an announcement, God himself will take Ira's spin on it," Heath argued before Matt accepted it as truth.

Back in the ballroom, the dance floor had been completely covered with enough seating for the immense crowd of reporters that were anticipated. Members of the media from virtually every major news source were expected to attend, especially numerous local and national gay news and culture magazines, which had sunk their teeth into the story as soon as it officially broke thirty-six hours earlier.

With only forty minutes before the three o'clock scheduled start time, Matt was nervously pacing in one of the hotel's bedrooms, which was serving as his place to prepare himself. He had wanted to avoid having to walk any sort of distance to the conference where he might have to face a gauntlet of reporters and cameras, so he had Ira arrange for the conference to be in a ballroom that was accessible directly from a private service elevator. Ira had complimented Matt on thinking about such an important detail, while at the same time yelling at his client for insisting that Heath hangout with him in the prep room and sit in on the press conference. Matt eventually convinced his agent, with the help of Taylor's promise to come along with her boyfriend, that after the interview there wouldn't be any more speculation.

Heath sat in a tattered and stained hotel armchair, watching his friend sweat through his second dress shirt of the afternoon.

"Is it getting hotter in here? Isn't the air-conditioning on?" Matt asked as he started to remove his now-soaked dark blue dress shirt.

"Dude, you have to calm down. I've turned that dial to solid blue. It's as cold as it's gonna get. The only way you're going to get any cooler is if we stuff you in a freezer. Why are you freaking out? You're not telling these people anything that they haven't already figured out. You're just setting everything straight, so to speak," Heath said, ignoring the look of dread that Matt shot him. "It's not going to help if you work yourself up so much that you go down there all hysterical."

"*Hysterical?* Damn, I wish I could calm down to be in hysterics. Unlike you, I recognize that this is my life, Heath. And it's over, everything is over! I might as well leave the team and League now."

"That's fucking bullshit, Matt, and you know it," Heath argued. "You're life isn't over. It's just changed. It's just less in the dark. Granted this isn't the way you wanted it to happen, but you can't actually hate the idea of not having to hide anymore."

"All I know is that from now on, I will be listed in the newspapers as 'Matt Walker, the gay basketball player."

"It's better than some other athletes' taglines," Heath said quickly. "You're not O.J. Simpson! Want to try out that baggage?"

"Are you smoking crack?" Taylor said, recoiling from her boyfriend's comment. "He's gay, not a nearly-convicted murderer!"

"I know that," Heath said, pointing to himself and then at Matt. "But he doesn't."

"Look, I know that I could have had a tougher set of circumstances to overcome," Matt conceded. "I come from an upper-class family. I'm well educated and I have more money than I know what to do with. Things could be worse, but it doesn't change the fact that I don't want to be famous just because I'm gay! I'm an athlete. I have the skills to be in the League. I don't want to be a special case."

"You're right. You do have the skills," Heath said. "But you are special, because you're the first one who will be openly gay. And as shitty as this sounds, you're going to be the subject of some ridicule. So you can either make amends by coming clean and setting an example for future professional gay athletes, or you can keep going down this perverse road you're on."

"I'm not nervous about the fact that I'm coming out. That cat's already out of the bag. I'm more nervous about my inability to not piss anyone off. In case you haven't been paying attention, I haven't exactly been too swift with the media lately, and that was when I was dealing with only one reporter."

"And that was also when you didn't know what you were going to say. We've talked about this Bro. You know what you have to do, if you want to resume your life."

"Heath, I can't resume my life. I want my life back. Because of all this, no matter what I say or do, everything is going to be different."

"Excuse me? Did I just hear that? Are you seriously trying to tell me that you want your life to go on the way it was? How many times did we empty a case of Sam Adams in the loft while I listened to you bitch about how you were tired of having meaningless relationships," Heath said as he flipped through the channels on the television, being sure to fly past ESPN's pre-press conference speculation roundtable. "You'd just sit there and explain that the only guys who ended up dating you were the ones who loved the fact that you seemed straight or played straight. If I remember correctly, I think you're favorite quote was 'I only attract liars who want to date other liars.'"

"Fine, you got me. My dating life has consistently sucked ass, but the rest of my life was in order. I got to play ball, I got to be me."

"You weren't being you. You were being what a marketing bobblehead doll on the twenty-fifth floor on Fifth Avenue needed you to be. But now, you can take control of this thing. You can go down there and tell them who exactly you are, and your life is yours. The media will have nothing on you anymore," Heath said, grabbing his best friend by the shoulders and shaking him slightly.

"How can you sit there and tell him to do this baby? Coming out could completely ruin everything he's built in his life?" Taylor asked, rubbing Matt's obviously tense shoulders.

"Because if he doesn't do something proactive about this, then all that stuff that you're talking about will just implode around him. Other people will do the talking for him, and basketball will be the last thing on his mind," Heath pleaded. "Matt, buddy, you just have to consider what you're saying to the media before you open your mouth. You know what your goal is now, and Ira has given you pointers on how to get there. Just relax and take care of this other shit, so you can resume your life and lead the Knicks into the playoffs tonight."

"Heath, I play basketball because the only thing that matters happens on the court. If you make a jump shot, you score. If you score more points than your opponent, you win. It's not politics and isn't full of intangibles I can't control or affect. I like that. Everything that happens out of bounds doesn't count."

"Well I'm sorry to tell you this, Matt," Heath said as he strolled across the floor, getting ready to join the gathering storm brewing ten stories below their room. "But you're not 14 years old playing in some youth league, so it's all about the intangibles. Out of bounds is in play in the real world. So, you need to finally let yourself step out of bounds."

*　　*　　*

"First, I would like to take this opportunity to apologize to the gay and lesbian community, which I deeply and regrettably offended with my behavior and my statements over the past twenty-four hours. While I cannot expect forgiveness from each one of you, I believe that you will all agree that every coming out story doesn't go exactly as planned."

The cameras clicked faster as nearly everyone in the room gasped in shock. The media corps then knew this press conference was no censure from the NBA or the Knicks management telling their young star to say sorry and then shut up. This was a coming out party.

"So, let me clear things up for you. I am a homosexual who plays in the National Basketball Association. While not everything that has been stated in the media has been the truth, that is the one undeniable fact that I cannot refute."

A press corps that had been expecting the chance to personally witness a star's meteoric fall from grace as a result of the League's expected reprimand, now sat utterly stunned, unsure of how they should proceed with something they were absolutely unprepared for.

As Matt continued with his short, prepared statement, allowing the others seated alongside him to make their own statements, the reporters worked themselves into a frenzy when Ira finally opened up the room for questions. Leonard, the reporter that had led Matt into his most publicized gaffe, boldly unleashed the first question. "Mr. Walker, you're saying, on the record, that you are a homosexual, and that you have not 'left that lifestyle' as you said yesterday??"

"That's exactly what I'm saying, Leonard. Honestly, I was under a lot of pressure and when I opened my mouth, that is what came out. It was an insanely inappropriate and untrue comment. It is my belief that sexual orientation is not a fluid concept and there is nothing that can be done to change it, no matter what you do."

"Why are you doing this now? Did the League pressure you to come out to repair the image of itself or the New York Knicks organization, which was damaged by your earlier comments?" asked an unfamiliar voice from the back of the ballroom.

"The NBA had nothing to do with my decision to hold this press conference, but I thank them for their support. After some serious soul searching on my part, and with the help of some very good friends, I came to the conclusion that I was being unfair to the League, my teammates, my fans, the gay community and mostly myself. My only option became clear—I had to announce my sexual orientation and get this over with."

"So the negative reaction brought about this decision? Do you think if you had said something earlier a lot of trouble could have been avoided?" asked ESPN's David Aldridge, the same man who covered Matt's rise to national prep school fame.

"I'm not going to lie to you," Matt said before giving away a little laugh at the irony. "I don't think I would have done this right now or ever if the current chain of events had not been set in motion. So, yes, the severity of the reactions to my ridiculous comments definitely helped seal the deal. But this is something I think I've secretly wanted to do for a while now. I was just not being honest with myself."

"Then why did it take so long?" shouted someone very near the podium.

"I decided a long time ago to keep my private life away from the public eye. I believed that you guys had no right to know what was going on in my personal life. Besides the fact that I believed it would hurt my career as a professional basketball player, I didn't truly understand the gray lines people use when dealing with celebrities and what is appropriate or inappropriate. Apparently this applies even to quasi-celebrities like myself."

"Were you afraid that people within the League wouldn't accept you if you came out? Are you still worried about that?" Kevin Ashbie asked.

"This is a very small community," Matt said, choosing his words carefully. "And it's always been true that people that are different from the norm standout more in these smaller groups. While I hope that my announcement doesn't change anything and that I will be judged by my performance on the court and not how I live my life off of it, I must concede that these people are just as human as I am. We are all going to slip up from time to time and not do the right thing every time. But I have to have faith. Many of the guys in the League have made their share of mistakes, even ones of a criminal nature, but they have still been embraced and promoted by the League and the fans . . ."

"So you think you'll be accepted by your teammates?" Kevin interrupted.

"The League has shown over and over again that it will accept you no matter how different you are as long as you can play ball. Bottom line is that everyone wants to win. I know coaches who would play the Devil himself, if he could chalk up another win for them. But I'm also a realist, and I know that some people will have major issues with what I'm announcing today."

"With your contract up this off-season, do you think you'll get resigned by the Knicks?" Leonard asked.

"Honestly, Leonard, I don't know. I'm sure you can argue that this will play a role in their decision to pursue me as I become a free agent, but I'm hoping that they will judge me from the job that I've done on the court."

From out of the shadows of the numerous cameras rolled a voice. It was unfamiliar, but its style wasn't. "You don't seem like you think this is a big deal and that we all should go 'Wow, he's gay, but that's fine 'cause he still thinks that he will be judged by whatever he does on the court.' Don't you think that's a little too idealistic?"

"I'm sorry," Matt said, searching for an answer as well as the body from which the voice came. "I don't know what you mean."

"I'm just saying," shouted a little man shouting from the back row, "that it seems like you want us all to cheer for you coming out and being the first gay basketball player."

"I don't think I'm asking you to do that at all," Matt responded before seeing the man whom he had been talking to walk through the crowd and not seem very comfortable with all the press in the stands.

"Oh come on!" the reporter shrieked. "It's not like you're even the first out gay athlete. I've done interviews with football, tennis, baseball, wrestling, and track and field athletes who are out. Isn't the only story here your choice to deny who you are for personal gain, all the while helping others to continue to vilify the gay community?"

The reporter looked smug as he collected odd glances from nearly everyone in the room. Matt could clearly see he was working for one of the national gay magazines, which would undoubtedly put Matt on the cover as soon as he gave a one-on-one interview. But now this reporter was playing the role of a bitter jaded queen, who probably was more personally jealous of the national attention Matt was getting for coming out than he was for sporting this season's Prada shoes.

Matt took a long pause and turned to Ira for a reassuring look before continuing, "First, I believe that I am now the first gay man to come out while still on the roster of a major sport's team. I do believe that is a big deal. Obviously, I'm not the first gay athlete to come out. But anyone who knows sports realizes that basketball is completely different from all of those sports. You mentioned mostly individual sports, but they're largely irrelevant to this issue since most people are perplexed by the idea of a gay man and straight man sharing a huddle. They don't care that much if gay men are staring at each other from across the net in tennis or climbing up the stairs after each other in diving or even waiting on their scores in gymnastics or figure skating. It's all about that machismo of the huddle and the traditional big three sports, where there has been such a taboo with gay men being out and proud."

Matt's mouth began to dry, but he was on a roll as the words that he had known, but were absent so many times before, finally came pouring forth. "Think about it, there has to be a reason why there are no professional athletes on a team sport that are out while they're still playing, let alone professional basketball players. The team sports are about trust, and sexuality is a divisive issue. Now, among the team sports, there isn't another as small as basketball. Only five on the floor, twelve on a squad. That creates an environment where being different makes it just a little harder to keep team harmony."

"So, you're saying that it's possible that you're the only gay man in the NBA?" asked the same peeved reporter.

"Of course it's possible. I don't think it's true, but I could definitely be the only case. All I'm saying is that basketball would have been the last place to experience a 'coming out' trend. All the speculation was on baseball, or even football. Not a word was spoken about basketball and I think that's because there's no more traditional locker room than the basketball locker room. It all plays into that smaller environment I just mentioned. Another reason is that basketball's culture is more urban and hip-hop, and to mainstream America that isn't a gay one. But let me tell you this. Gay men are everywhere. We are just like everyone in this room in that we are just as complex and diverse as you."

As applause peppered the press conference, Matt noticed Heath smiling brightly, standing alongside Taylor. He wished that Reese was there and was asking him these tough questions. He didn't want to continue his own coming out story without the boyfriend he wanted to be at his side throughout the entire process.

After League officials and Coach Baker answered a few of the questions from the floor, Matt made a motion to Ira to close out the press conference. But another volley of inquiries commenced. "You said you don't think it's true that you are the only gay man in the NBA, why do you think that? Do you know some others? Do you date within the League?" asked an expressive reporter from the *Post's* gossip pages.

"No, I don't know of anyone else in the League. Even if I did I don't think . . ."

"Is Henry Fielding or Reese Gibbons your boyfriend?" she followed up, interrupting Matt, while simultaneously soliciting quite a few groans from the other reporters and most of the members of the panel on stage. Matt, however, kept a wide smile on his face and responded quickly, loving the fact that Ira had prepared him specifically on this question.

"Mr. Fielding and I were, at one time, involved. Currently, however, we are not, and you can bet that after his little stunt we won't be again anytime soon."

"And Reese Gibbons?" demanded the gossip writer.

Matt exhaled deeply and answered, "I don't think I can answer that question."

Chapter Twenty

The locker room that afternoon was reminiscent of a frat house the morning after a Friday night kegger. The only movement in the musk saturated space came from a few of the trainers scurrying about, trying to get the players to loosen up and stretch before hitting the court for warm-ups. Despite Matt's admission of his sexuality, unbelievably, no one seemed to care much or show a hint of interest in anything but that evening's game.

The first person that took it upon himself to approach Matt was Coach Baker. Matt noticed his coach crossing the locker room from his office and immediately took note of the less-than-enthusiastic look plastered on his coach's face. As the old man sat himself down on a seat beside him, Matt braced himself for what he expected to be a lecture about respecting the position that the team was in currently and seizing every opportunity that lay out before him. It was an oldie but goodie from Coach Baker's grab bag of clichéd coaching speeches.

"Well Walker, I don't know what to say to you," he said, hanging his head.

"Coach, I'm sorry about earlier. I cleared it with the front office, as well as the League. I know I should have talked to you about it beforehand, but my agent was pretty damn convincing that I needed to come out now before this thing totally exploded. I'm sorry, again, if I put you in a bad position."

"Oh forget that," the man said, swatting his hand away as if to throw out the last day and a half in Knick history. "You didn't have to clear that with me. This is your life. I'm just going to say

I had no idea you were such a hard ass. You've been shooting lights out, knowing the whole time that this was probably going to break sometime soon. To do what you did today, that took some balls Walker."

"Thanks Coach." Matt said, surprised yet encouraged from the support.

"What? You thought I was gonna lay into you? Look Walker, lately you've done nothing but help this team, and for that you have my full support," he said while looking around the locker room, careful to avoid eye contact. "And I think you have the support of most of the team. These guys are all professional. I know they respect the skills you bring to the court. Hell, I know at least four of them have talked to the front office telling them to keep you, and that was after your little speech across the street. So you just keep doing what you've been doing, and don't let some of the trash in the stands get to you too much." The coach stood up from his place on the bench beside his now-immensely famous player, patted him on the back and walked to the other side of the locker room to talk to his starting center.

Watching his coach walk away, Matt thought what a great coach and team he was surrounded by. Their silence was encouragement enough as they all stayed on task. But with Coach Baker, he certainly had not expected the man to bench him or try to force him off the team, but he definitely didn't anticipate getting more than a pat on the back. Continuing to think about what Coach Baker had just said, Matt sat at his locker and continued his pre-game routine of stretching and listening to Parliament's "Mothership Connection," which had been his pregame album of choice since he was playing basketball at White Hall Academy.

On the CD's second track, Matt found Wayne sidled up next to him. "How are you holdin' up?"

"Not too bad."

"Shit, Casper, you look ah'right. But I never heard you blast Mr. Clinton that loud. I was standin' at my crib and heard George from your 1984 old school phones. I mean, fuck Casper, you in the League. You can spend more than two-fifty on some earphones."

Matt laughed off Wayne's constant digs into his style while he heard his friend continue to lower his voice and continue, "You sure you all right, tho? It couldn't have been that bad in there." Unbeknownst to Matt, Wayne had been sitting in the back of the ballroom throughout the press conference.

"It was nothin' I want to put in my Christmas card," Matt said, trying to stay strong. "But it's kinda fucked up when you just stand there and watch your private life be discussed by a thousand reporters."

"Oh, that conference coulda been a lot worse, dog," Wayne said, shaking his head from side to side. "None of those people really cared anyway, they were just covering their own asses for their bosses. Judging from the look on our boss's face, I don't think you got anything to worry about."

"I should never even have worried about Coach or most of the guys on the team, and really, they're the last of my worries. Hell, even the front office doesn't seem to really care. What I'm freaking out about is what should I expect when we run through that tunnel tonight?"

"Sure you do," he said with a big smile. "You expect Pierce to stay up tight and not let you get your shot off. He won't respect your drive, so you gonna have to take it to him. And you expect him to think that he's God walkin' on water, when all he really is, is a player who shoots thirty times a night and makes less than half."

"Shit, I know that. I'm talking about the crowd. What are they going to be like?"

Wayne rolled his head from the left to his right and leaned back into the chair he'd stolen from Twan's locker. Now with his arms crossed and tucked under his armpits, he said, "They'll be loud. They'll cheer and they'll expect us to win, just like every New York crowd."

"Handles, what the fuck? Do you think I'm stupid?"

"No, you ain't stupid, but you're being a dumbass! Those

people out there, these people in here and everyone else doesn't give a shit what happened at three o'clock across the street! They don't care if you suck dick, or take it up the ass. All they care about is what you can do on the court. This is a simple game, Casper. Put the ball in the hoop more than the other guys and go home with a 'W.' Forget about everything else, it doesn't matter anymore. Control what you can and help us get that 'W.'"

*   *   *

The arena was rocking as the New York Knicks were about to take the court. Earlier during warm-ups the crowd was sparse and seemed like it was on Valium, which pleased Matt. He was able to get through his shooting drills with ease while ignoring the rare jabs at his sexuality.

After the team had gone back into the locker room for some final words from Coach Baker and another round of touch-ups on the ankle tapings from the athletic trainers, the press conference from earlier that day was played for the crowd on the JumboTron hanging above the court. Usually the crowd could be heard from the Knicks locker room as everyone stumbled to their seats, but this time there was an eerie silence permeating the thick concrete of the arena.

Matt couldn't decide if the silence was from the disgust the crowd was feeling or from just being stunned at the news coming from their starting shooting guard. He hoped that it was the latter and Wayne and Twan both came over and offered an encouraging pat on the back. But once the taped press conference ended and a video montage of the season began showing the resolve of this year's Knicks squad, the crowd perked up to the point where Matt hadn't heard more boos and more jeers than when the Celtics took the court moments before the treasured home team.

As the Knicks took the court to a standing ovation, a constant clapping and cheering took hold of the crowd as the latest techno version of Frank Sinatra's classic "New York, New York" rained from the speakers. The ovation continued as the team went into their final preparations for the start of their final regular season game.

When it came to introductions, Wayne and Twan led the way, garnering nothing but a euphoric blast from the stands. But when Matt was announced, it seemed nearly everyone in the crowd didn't really know what to do. There were some cheers while some people continued with their cries of hate. Matt tried to shrug it off, praying they were as confused as he was and hoped the officials would get the game started as quickly as possible.

But once the ball was in the air and the game was on its way, Matt settled down into his position as a basketball player and not as some freakish pop culture reference that was consuming the nation's media. His opponent wasn't about to let up on Matt as the Celtics' Paul Pierce was gunning for a forty-point performance in hopes of winning the League's Most Valuable Player award and the League's scoring title. Matt was unable to stop him as he lit up the first quarter for twelve points as the Knicks fell into an early eight point deficit.

Twan was ruling the paint and was managing to fend off the entire Celtics' frontcourt on sheer determination as he piled on twenty-three points before five minutes remained in the second half when the Knicks called a greatly needed timeout. "What the hell is happening out there?" Coach Baker barked at his players who fought to keep eye contact with their coach. "It's like none of you want to play anymore. You all want to pack it in. Is that what you want?"

No one responded and the coach drew up a play for inbounding the ball. Matt was to pass the ball directly into the low post to Twan, who would either take a shot or pitch it around to Wayne who would be cutting to the basket. As the team broke the huddle, Twan grabbed Matt's jersey and said, "Take the ball to hole!"

The Celtics defense was playing off Matt not allowing him to inbound the ball by double teaming the closest cutter to sideline. Finally as he was about to be called for a five-second violation, Matt found an opening and bounced the ball to Twan. As the entire Boston team converged on him, Twan kicked the ball to Wayne. Wayne fumbled the ball when a defender slapped it from his grasp and Matt was the closest to it. He quickly gobbled it up, sidestepped Pierce and went baseline towards the bucket. Before even thinking of what he was going to do, Matt had dunked the ball cleanly, giving the crowd something to cheer about.

From then on, Matt attacked the basket at will, drawing Pierce into foul trouble and eventually a seat on the bench. When the final seconds ticked off the clock, the Knicks had surged ahead of the visiting Celtics to claim a 125-102 victory. Matt had turned it on and scored forty-two points in a game every New York fan labeled a "must win" for the franchise.

The crowd was ecstatic and filled the court to be closer to their heroes. Finally, a chant began, "RE-SIGN MATT! RE-SIGN MATT! RE-SIGN MATT!"

* * *

As the majority of the Knicks players and staff pushed their way through the crowd that had gathered to celebrate the win clinching the final spot in the playoffs, Matt jogged through the tunnel towards their locker room amidst the still constant cheers for the team.

Entering the locker room, which had been covered in plastic to protect it from the anticipated spraying of champagne, each of the teammates exchanged handshakes, embraces and congratulations. Matt had just finished enthusiastically trading chest thumps with Wayne when he turned around to find another teammate to praise and came face to face with Anthony.

After looking Matt up and down Anthony said, "Looks like you got what you wanted, ain't no way you not gonna get signed after tonight. Gots to keep the fans happy. That's all the owners care about. I'll be all right though, I made sure of that."

Staring at Anthony with a look full of both astonishment and anger Matt let loose a tirade against the man who he no longer had the patience left to deal with. "What the fuck are you saying?

Were you the asshole who told Ashbie about my life? What? Couldn't handle the competition for your spot? Decided to try and use my life against me?"

As Matt continued to get even more enraged he began to ever so slightly push Anthony backwards into a row of lockers. Seeing the argument beginning to approach a physical level, Wayne quickly jumped behind his friend and held him back.

"I don't know what the fuck you smoking, White Bread. I could give a shit about who you shaggin'," Anthony shouted in Matt's face. "I don't waste my time with minor league reporters like that *Post* be-yatch. I had my face on the SI cover and the ESPN cover, I don't need his shitty play-by-play."

Matt was in a state of shock from Anthony's explanation and had to be held up by Wayne. He tried to utter some sort of apology but couldn't.

"Shit man, you really think it's that big a deal?" Anthony continued. "My contract is bank. I can sit on the bench and watch you play, and still watch my benjamins roll in. They wanna get rid of me, that's fine. Plenty of teams will want to pick me up. Everybody knows 'bout my skills."

"I'm sorry Anthony," Matt said meekly.

Anthony just cocked his head in acknowledgement and walked off towards the showers. Matt dropped to the bench behind him and sat in silence, no longer able to participate in the revelry that had consumed the rest of the team. Matt couldn't focus on anything other than the fact that now he had no possible suspects of who would have wanted to complicate his life. Matt's moment of sulking, however, was disrupted by Wayne grabbing him under the arms and lifting him up.

"Come on dog, let's get cleaned up and get out of here. We can grab dinner and get ready for Orlando. Ya know, we're in the postseason, baby!" Wayne said, smiling and trying to cheer up his friend and teammate.

The whole time he stood under the stream of scalding water, Matt couldn't get the question of who had really outed him from his mind. They hadn't gotten much of the facts right, in fact the only thing that was right about the initial story was that he was gay. He had never invited random boys back to his room, and he wasn't exactly a screamer in the bedroom. Whoever had decided to mess with him, had wanted things to go very public.

As Wayne and he walked out of the players' exit, Matt took a deep breath, filling his lungs with the air from a perfect spring evening. The long, hard winter had ended and he had survived. But despite the fact that Wayne had told him to drop the subject several times, Matt continued with his ravings about Anthony as they hoped into Wayne's black Cadillac Escalade.

"I can't believe it wasn't him! He's the only person who shouldn't want me to play next year. I just can't imagine who else that travels with us would have any reason to talk to the press."

"Jesus Matt, what good is it going to do you to know who did it? It's done, you're out, move on. You can't let figuring this out distract you. We basically start a whole new season in two days, you need to focus on Orlando and just let everything else settle down."

Matt thought about what Wayne was telling him as the duo headed downtown along Seventh Avenue. He decided that he really didn't feel like going somewhere that he might garner more attention or make any sort of scene, so he asked Wayne if he could just take him home.

Wayne guided his ride across 14th Street as he turned to Matt when they stopped at a traffic light. "I did it Matt. I told Kevin about you."

"You? What the fuck? Why in God's name did you do this?" Matt screamed while nearly hurling himself at his friend.

"I told him because I am your friend. Think about it Matt. The way things are going, you're gonna be big," Wayne argued while staring directly at Matt. "I mean this won't be our only trip to the playoffs, or your first multimillion-dollar contract extension. You're gonna be the great white hope of the NBA. Just think how it would have been if you were outed after the League put you on every billboard between here and Philly."

Matt sat speechless as the light turned green and Wayne continued driving south into the West Village. "And did you plan on being single for the rest of your life?" he asked. "I don't think you did, and if I'm right that means that this would have happened eventually. It could have broke in the middle of the Finals. It could have happened next year or the year after that. But it would have happened. This way it happened now before it could tarnish some image the League gave you, and it started with a pro reporter who had no facts. You eventually got to control the story, once you stopped fuckin' the shit up, dawg. But the ball was still in your court the whole time."

"Why didn't you wait till the end of the season? Why did you make me have to deal with it now?"

"I did it 'cause now you can answer the critics on the court," Wayne said confidently as if he had planned this conversation all along. "If it broke this summer, which it easily could have, you wouldn't have gotten signed. This way you can show that you bein' gay has no effect on your game."

Matt smiled as he bought into his friend's argument, while still wanting to smash Wayne's head into the center console. "Look, I also ain't stupid, Matt. I knew that something had happened with Reese. I knew you fucked things up, like you had with all the others. And while you were still playing better than most white boys I've seen, eventually it was gonna start to affect that too."

"Damn, and I thought someone was trying to fuck with me. You could have told me sooner, or given me some sort of warning," Matt replied, starting to smile again.

"Man, I just want you to enjoy what's gonna start happenin' to you, and I thought the only way that was going to happen was if you weren't hiding anymore. Now go ahead and start playin' with someone you know you care about."

Matt rocked forward from Wayne sharply hitting his brakes, stopping the SUV in front of Matt's loft. He turned to his friend for an explanation of his horrible driving skills, but only found Wayne looking toward Matt's building and smiling. Matt turned again following Wayne's stare and immediately saw Reese standing by the building's door.

"Go play, Casper."

Printed in the United States
22172LVS00002B/67-72